AF484050

A Woman's Guide to True Crime

Mary Thorson

Rock and a Hard Place Press

Published by Rock and a Hard Place Press, an imprint of Rock and a Hard Place Press, LLC,
Woodbridge, NJ.
rockandahardplacemag.com
amazon.com/~/e/B08WPQG5YV

Printed in the United States of America

"In this dark, unsettling collection, Thorson imagines long-ago crimes, from brutal multiple murders to a deadly hotel blaze. Like Elizabeth Brundage and Joyce Carol Oates, Thorson maps the darkness where violence intersects with ordinary life. Her narrators are lovers, neighbors, children, criminals, and victims—and often something in-between. The stories move through space and time, spanning nearly a century, without breaking the spell of Thorson's understated, assured voice. Like the images in dreams, fragments of this uncanny story collection dwell hauntingly in my mind."
—Kelsey Rae Dimberg, author of *Girl in the Rearview Mirror* and *Snake Oil*

"A lesser writer would have failed these characters, but Mary Thorson does the unimaginable here: she captures, with dignity and grace and tenderness, those who must live in the wake of tragedy and horror. A profoundly moving collection that seeks to illuminate our sheer will to go on in the face of what seems insurmountable."
—Keith Rosson, author of *Coffin Moon* and *Fever House*

"***A Woman's Guide to True Crime*** is a crystal ball showing our past, and our future. Thorson is eerily prescient, her prose surprising like a deep cut from a butter knife. The storytelling is uncomfortable, revealing, and completely original and the collection is unlike anything on the shelves. I loved it."
—Meagan Lucas, author of the Anthony nominated collection *Here in the Dark*, and Editor in Chief of *Reckon Review*

DEDICATION

This book is for my mom, because I miss her.

Contents

1. The Cold Gets In   1
    Milwaukee, WI. 1952

2. Casadastraphobia   18
    Skidmore, MO. 1973-1981

3. Daughters of Fire   36
    Milwaukee, WI. 1883

4. Maneater   55
    Manhattan, NY. 1916

5. She Goes First   68
    New York City, NY. 1928

6. Sunvalley Mall, 1985   81

7. Love Me Tender   84
    Chicago, IL. 1956

8. The Book of Ruth   105
    Kirtland, OH. 1989

9.   In German, Hörst Du Das Means 'Do You Hear
     That?'
     Hinterkaifeck, Germany. 1922   121

10. Moonlight Madness   126
     Texarkana, AR. 1946

11. Mom & Dad's Bed   144
     San Bernardino, CA. 1964

12. Cabin 28   151
     Keddie, CA. 1981

13. Undark   164
     Ottawa, IL. 1930

14. The Hive Broke on a Sunday   180
     Franklin Township, NJ. 1922

15. Playing House   191
     Lincoln, NE. 1958

16. Wonderland   198

Acknowledgements   216

About the Author   220

Chapter One

The Cold Gets In

Milwaukee, WI. 1952

The morning after the Schulz murders, Betsy and her father sat in the back of St. Hedwig's so they could leave right after communion. Before they had left for church, her father had been looking over the paper. He asked her, in his low mumbling so she needed to come closer to hear, Don't you know him? He kept a dirty finger on the paper, right underneath the headline: *Family Members Murdered, Teen Son Missing*. Betsy felt a wave of dread travel the length of her body, almost pulsating, and she tried to grab the page.

"I'm not done, yet," he said, pulling it closer to his face.

She leaned against the kitchen counter and waited for him. Then, he folded up the paper, set it down, and went to the front hall to get ready. She read it as fast as she could before he came in saying they had to go. The words only registering as flashes as her father walked back into the kitchen: *Katherine, 38, found*

1

in the kitchen. Robert, 11, found underneath the bed. Kathleen, 6, found in the closet. John, 16, missing.

"It's time, now," Betsy's father said.

They ducked into the back pew like intruders, and when it came time for communion, they marched slowly up the aisle. She pressed the wafer to the roof of her mouth with her tongue and held it there. You're not supposed to chew Christ, her father told her once, so she would let it melt and become like a plastic coating. They were almost to their front door by the time it was gone. Going to church wasn't something they did until after Betsy's mother died the year before—so Betsy wasn't all that familiar with the routine, but she knew sneaking out like this was disrespectful. She could feel the whole church watching her leave.

***

The next day at school, Linda Lepinski was waiting by their shared gym locker to tell Betsy they had found John Schulz.

She put a hand on Betsy's arm, as if what she had said was meant to be consoling. Betsy stood still with her dress in her hand, wanting desperately to bury her face in it. The echoes of conversation that had been bouncing around the locker room became quieter. The other girls were closing their lockers slowly, in order to hear.

"He's been arrested," she said, like an apology.

They caught John in Missouri after he stopped at a diner for breakfast. As Linda kept talking, Betsy wondered if, at any point between the car ride and the coffee at the diner, if maybe he had stopped at a phone booth. He knew her number by heart. He had told her so. She remembered when she first told it to him. She'd watched him write it down the length of his arm.

"Did you know?" Linda asked.

"Know what? Betsy whispered.

"I mean." Linda squirmed. "Did he say anything?"

She hadn't asked this last question quietly enough. Betsy felt like her skin had been set on fire. The corners of her eyes started to sting from an effort not to blink. Linda's hand was back on her arm, and when she tried to rub it reassuringly, Betsy jerked herself away. She just missed hitting her hand against her locker—though she braced for the metallic pop, anyway.

***

When John first asked Betsy out, he wanted her to watch the sunset with him on the beach. Betsy couldn't tell if the hairs on his upper lip were for lack of trying or lack of growth. She thought she might be able to count them all and the end result would be somewhere under fifty. She had to work at the theater that night, but she wanted him to ask.

"Not really," she said.

"Why not?" John took a step back.

"I don't really have the time to wait for Earth to flip its rotation." She waited for a second. She wanted him to get the joke.

"Lake Michigan is east," she said.

"Your parents don't let you go down there or something?"

"No. Not that. Lake Michigan is east and the sun sets in the west. You can't watch the sunset from the lake."

"Sure you can, I've done it plenty," John said.

"From Lake Michigan?"

"Sure," John said.

"Then you must be some kind of Greek god, like Apollo."

"Who?"

"Apollo, god of the sun," Betsy said.

"Well, do you want to or not?"

"Do you even know my name?" Betsy asked.

"Do you know mine?"

"Yeah—Apollo, I just told you. Everyone knows who you are."

And they did. John Schulz had transferred over to Riverside in the beginning of the year. He had been expelled from his old school, and everyone knew that, too. But, for what, the rumors ran wild. Someone said he sent a kid to the hospital with a broken back after he threw him down the stairs. Someone else said that he punched one of his teachers after they had held him in detention. Someone said he brought a knife to school. Someone said it was a gun. Someone said he had tried to burn the school down. Betsy was too afraid to ask.

***

A few days after, Betsy was walking with her father up the steps of St. Hedwig's when John appeared behind them. He tried to talk to her father, who hadn't even noticed he was there.

"I go to school with your daughter over at Riverside," John was saying with his hand out, slipping in front of them.

"Okay," her father said, not taking his hands out of his pockets.

"Daddy, this is John Schulz."

"He said so."

"Well, anyway, I was wondering if I might take your daughter out sometime, sir?"

"Mass is starting, Betsy." Her father walked ahead, keeping his head down while he got in the door as it was closing behind someone.

Betsy pulled at her hair nervously while John tried to gather himself.

"Hard man, I guess," John said.

"Not hard, I don't think. I guess—well, it's difficult to explain."

"Doesn't like me much, easy to tell that."

Betsy touched John's arm and he took a step down to be closer to her.

"No, he's just not interested . . . in anything. He doesn't really care one way or another about anything."

"So he wouldn't care if I called you sometime?"

***

At the lake, Betsy moved her hand along the rock in order to reach his. The sun was going down on their backs and Betsy had to squint when she looked at him. His breath came out frozen and he was trying not to shake with cold as the wind burned up their faces. The beach was all white. The icecaps had trapped the waves and she could only hear the echo of them moving underneath.

"This was stupid. I shouldn't have brought you here. You must think I'm some kind of idiot. A real jerk."

"Actually, did you know that it's warmer by the lake than anywhere else?"

"You're smart, huh?" He was annoyed, and she didn't know what he wanted, but she wanted to know.

"Not really."

"Don't lie. I'm sure you get straight A's. Perfect student and all that."

"I don't. I promise." Betsy was lying.

He knew it somehow. He rolled his eyes and started looking off in different directions like he had to get somewhere else.

"I don't know how to drive a car." She almost shouted it. Despite the cold, her face flushed and her armpits started to dampen.

"What?" Aloof, as if he hadn't heard her just fine.

"I don't know how to drive. My dad's never taken me out. I'm 16, I should be driving like everyone else, but I've never even gone down an alley."

"How come he doesn't take you?"

"I don't know. He's never asked, so I don't ask."

"I'm a good driver, you know," he sniffed, the snot running from his nose. "I might show you some things."

"Really?"

"Sure. I guess."

"That'd be great. It's embarrassing, really."

"My dad sometimes lets me take out the car, but when he's out it's just my mom and she yells and screams at me like a real bitch."

She had never heard anyone describe a mother like this. Betsy thought of how hard it was for her mother to breathe, at the end.

"But, anyway, I don't care. I just take it whenever I want it."

"You get in trouble?"

He shrugged. "Yeah—but who cares, you know? It doesn't matter."

And she knew it didn't.

***

He would take her out for driving lessons, but Betsy would never get out of the passenger seat. She didn't think he would ever let her move over, but she really didn't mind. The two of them sat on the bench seat of Arno Schulz's Kaiser Deluxe. John twisted around the radio knob but the car wasn't on yet so all it did was make a clicking sound.

"I asked my dad if I could take his, even though it's new. Look here." He gripped the knob of the gear shift, and Betsy kept her hands tucked between her thighs.

"It's manual," he said. "Lots harder for girls. My mom made him get her an automatic, even though manual's more fun. My dad says that's when you're really driving."

John was smiling and Betsy felt like she was spying on him.

"Put your hand on top of mine." Without asking, John reached for her. His bare knuckles swept the inside of her thigh, his dry skin scraping against her nylons. Betsy held that feeling in the breath inside her mouth. He placed her hand on top of his so her fingers fit between his fingers. They both looked at their hands and waited for the other one to do something.

"Try shifting up to first," John said softly.

She pushed the gear forward, but it wouldn't budge. Her hand slid hard against his.

"It won't go," she said.

"Shoot, sorry. I forgot—I forgot to press the clutch down. Sorry." John laughed and stomped his foot on the pedal. "This is how my dad taught me. He had me sit up next to him in front, even if my mom was in the car—well sometimes. He let me shift while he was driving starting when I was eight years old."

"My dad never lets me do anything at all. You're lucky," she said.

"Yeah, right." John rolled his eyes. "Watch this." With his foot still on the clutch, he slipped the gear into neutral. Betsy felt the muscles and tendons get tighter underneath her limp fingers. Little blue veins had appeared in-between his knuckles. She hadn't noticed that the car was moving until after she felt his eyes on her, waiting for her to react. So she did. She squealed a little and from the look on his face that seemed to be what he wanted.

***

The Friday night before the murders, John's hand was sweaty when he put it on top of her thigh. Betsy could feel the dampness through the tiny holes in her nylons. He had cut the engine right when Johnny Ray was belting *"So go on baby and cry."* When it was suddenly silenced, the air in the car seemed muffled, as if someone who had been screaming was stopped. John's pinky was moving against the hem of her black woolen skirt like it had an itch. Betsy studied his little nail that was short but with a crooked edge because he had chewed it. Betsy had noticed those little white specks on his nails, like her father's, but she never saw them on her own.

John had crept underneath now and his fingertips started to press on the inside of her thigh and she hated it. In church, when she would sit herself down on the hard pew, Betsy would watch the fat of her thighs spread out to either side and meet flush in the middle. They would sweat no matter how cold the church was. They were sweating now, and it was cold.

John wasn't looking at her. He was watching his hand. His nose began to run and he sniffed. Betsy wanted to give him the tissue she had in her pocket, but she didn't want to move—afraid that she would scare him off. His dry lips were slightly parted and Betsy could see his breath falling out of his mouth. She opened her own mouth hoping she would suck in some of his air.

"It's okay," he said, but she didn't believe him.

She put her hand on his, which was now completely hiding under her skirt, and she spread her thighs apart—almost able to hear the tear between them.

***

She hadn't said no. Not exactly. She had told him "maybe later."

He showed up at the theater hours after the killings. From the ticket booth she could see him crossing the street while two of his friends waited by his mother's car, not the good one. John had started jogging across Farwell Avenue but once he saw Betsy watching him he slowed down to a strut. He didn't speed up when a car turned onto the street and its headlights lit him up. In that unforgiving yellow light, Betsy could see how pale he was. She thought that he seemed angry and on edge by the way he was coming. It was almost as though he were barreling towards her, though he was going so determinedly slow.

"Hi, there," she said to him.

As if he hadn't expected her to be there, he cocked his head and flashed something close to a smile. He leaned against the window and kept his hands in his pockets.

"Hi, yourself," he said, pointing his chin in Betsy's direction.

"You all here to see a movie?" she asked.

The only thing they had showing was some cartoon picture that she knew John wouldn't be caught dead seeing.

"No, I don't think so. What are you doing tonight?"

Betsy screwed up her face. She could see how ugly it looked in her reflection in the glass so she quickly straightened it out and smiled at him.

"What do you mean?" she asked.

"Just asking you a question. What—are—you—doing?"

He sounded it out for her, slowly and mean. Betsy tightened up her eyebrows and stared at him. He shrugged up into his coat a little more and didn't look at her straight.

"I'm working. You see I'm in here, right?"

"Alright. I meant later, okay?"

"Sure," she said.

"So? What about later?"

"I don't know, it'll be midnight when I get off."

"And what?" he asked.

"My dad'll be waiting for me to come home."

"You lie. Your dad is probably dead asleep right now. He won't even hear you come in."

"I don't know, I don't think so. Not tonight. Why not tomorrow?"

"Please, tonight, Bets? Okay?"

His hands were out of his pockets and gripping the tiled counter that wrapped around the little room she was in. He was breathing hard, as if he was gasping for air, as if his shoulders had just become incredibly heavy and they were weighing down his lungs. His eyes were wide open. The amount of white showing was unnerving. They were watering but he wouldn't blink; even if he wanted to, he was willing himself not to, Betsy was sure of it. He was frozen there.

"Maybe later, then," she said.

"Yeah?" He smiled and something inside him seemed to shift and let go. Like he might cry, it was the saddest looking smile Betsy had ever seen.

"Yeah, maybe," she said.

"Okay, then. I'll come back later—midnight. We're going to the game, but that'll get out earlier."

"Fine."

John pressed his palm against the glass and held it there. That pathetic smile was still on his face. Betsy knew she should respond in some sweet way that might alleviate him, but she didn't. One of his friends reached into the car and honked the horn. John took his hand off the glass as if it had burnt him. He walked back to the car and then drove off.

Later, she waited for him. For a few minutes, she watched her boss lock up the main office and turn off the lights in the lobby. She was on an uncomfortable wooden bench keeping an eye out for a car that might pull up outside and park underneath the marquee. The lights were still running. Betsy had always thought of the moving light as one living thing that jumped from lightbulb to lightbulb, like a ghost possessing the glass one moment and then leaving it empty the next. Having burned everything up, it would just move on. Her boss came over and asked if she needed a ride. She told him that she didn't; she was waiting for somebody who'd be there soon.

It was a quarter past midnight and she knew that John wasn't coming back.

"Well, I have to turn out the lights. Are you sure you don't need a ride?"

"I'm sure."

He stared at her for a second then turned them off. They faded orange like burning embers. It would have been better if she had just left with John when he came, she thought.

Later, John told the police he had a good time at the game, mostly—until the end. The screams bothered him, but he stayed until it was over.

***

After that Monday at school, she sat silent at the kitchen table. Her father was eating and she could hear his jaw popping every time he chewed. Her mother would talk over it during dinner because she hated the sound, long stories about nothing just to get to the end of the meal. Betsy was expecting the thing to become completely unhinged one day, and she knew that would be her problem. When he was done he rubbed his face with his big hand and sighed.

"That boy was bad," her father said, finally.

Betsy's cheeks flushed red.

"I knew that when I met him. You can tell about that kind of evil."

"You didn't know," came from her ragged throat.

"Maybe not all people can tell, but sharp ones can." Her father tapped his forehead.

"And you tell me now, then?"

"Not my business," he said.

"Not your business—" she swept her hand in front of herself, accidentally knocking the coffee pot to the floor.

Betsy watched it shatter and spill out over the black and red tiles. He didn't even react to the sound. He kept his eyes lazily open and fixed on her. Betsy pushed back her chair so it would scrape against the floor and grabbed the rag from the oven. She got on her hands and knees and started to clean the mess, but the harder she wiped, the more it spread, with coffee grounds like rocks scratching the tile.

"Yeah, with some people, you can just know it," he said.

She kept wiping until the mess was all around them.

****

She dreamt about John that night. Except, when she dreamt, she wasn't herself—she was him. She asked his mother for the car. She went upstairs. She got the shotgun. She asked, again, for the car. She called his mother by her first name, "Kathy," because that's what John had done. She pulled the trigger and felt the recoil push into her shoulder while she watched Mrs. Schulz collapse on the kitchen floor. She stalked through the house after John's brother and sister. She paused over the girl because he had done that. When she woke up she still felt trapped there in his skin—but not in his skin. In her own.

****

The day they brought John back from Missouri, hundreds of people were at the train station, but Betsy didn't see anyone there that she knew. A lot of reporters stood around, talking to each other, smiling and laughing. She felt as though someone was walking over her grave—or his. She wanted to get closer, but the crowd was too thick. Too many elbows ready to jab out to protect vantage points. Betsy didn't have a chance. She stood shorter than the majority of the crowd. Her height had been a thing John liked. It was a joke that John liked to play, him being so tall and her so short; he'd prop his arm up on top of her head and rest it there, saying "you're just right, Bets." The air was thin down where she was in the crowd, so Betsy stood up on her toes and took a deep breath. A flash went off. Someone shouted his name. Then it was like a lightning storm. She heard it, over and over again. His name. Why'd you do it, John? All those strangers asking why'd you do it, John? Why'd you kill your mom, John? Why'd you kill the kids?

She couldn't see him behind all those people, but the general direction of the crowd began to shift and she knew where he was. He was like a magnet. Betsy was pulled with the crowd. She wanted to be facing him dead on if she could get a look at him. The flashes didn't stop, and she thought she could see the top of his head, the lights bouncing off his straight black hair shining with grease. Then, there was a gap in the crowd, and there he was. Pale, but making a strange face—the sort of smile you have when you're not supposed to have one at all. She couldn't quite tell, but she thought maybe he could see her. She had the sudden urge to stick her hand up and wave at him. She opened her mouth to yell for him, but then his face changed. He looked like a wounded animal, trying to hide when cornered. He turned and dipped his head and the crowd moved toward the doors. Outside she could see the police car waiting with its lights already on. The flashes kept going and were hitting the windows making it hard for her to see it when John fit all of his awkward limbs in the back. Suddenly everyone scattered.

There was a giant noise that gradually got quieter as they fled the station. In a matter of seconds, she was almost alone in the room. The ticket takers stood wide-eyed at their stations.

A stuttering boarding announcement came over the loudspeaker and finally, she started toward the doors. When she stepped outside, the wind hit her with a breathtaking force. She hunched her shoulders up to her ears and started walking towards the Wisconsin Ave. bus. It was a barren darkness, the kind of night that makes the world empty and sharp. When she reached the bus, the driver wasn't in it. The keys were gone and there was a sign hanging over the steering wheel: Bathroom Break, back in 10.

She stood in the aisle, looking over the rows of empty seats. Finally, she walked to the back and sat in the dark. The light from the street lamps glowed outside, but didn't make it in. The wind rocked the bus, slipping in through the door and loose windowpanes. Betsy unbuttoned her coat and pulled her knees into her chest, then buttoned it back up over them. She bowed her head and breathed into the inside of her jacket. She thought about the warmth inside his dad's car. You see? It's like this, he would say.

In Milwaukee, WI in 1952, John Schulz, 16, murdered his mother, brother, and sister while his father was out of town. He told police it was over being able to attend a high school basketball game and his mom not letting him borrow the car.

From TIME, *"I wrote a note to my father . . . It*

said: 'Sorry things have happened this way. Maybe we will meet again . . . Your Twisted Son.' Then I drove toward Geneva, Illinois. I followed [Route] 66."
–John Schulz

Chapter Two

Casadastraphobia

Skidmore, MO. 1973-1981

Trena got a strange feeling whenever she went outside. She thought, somehow, she might be taken up into the sky. Singularly pulled up into space without warning, and nothing would hold her to the ground. She'd be there alone, floating up into the dark, until she was so far away from Earth that she couldn't see it anymore. She knew she wouldn't be able to do anything to stop it, so she would purposefully walk underneath things; Trees, awnings, bridges. She even felt better if she wore baseball hats that kept the top of her head from being exposed. She never told anyone about this. Saying it out loud would do one of two things; they would laugh at her and think she was nuts, or, saying the thing would make it real and when the last word of it left her mouth, she would lift off of the ground. She looked at her tennis shoes and thought about frantically kicking until they fell off her feet, returning to the earth as she kept going up.

She was walking in the shade the day she met Ken McElroy outside the school. He parked in his newest pick-up truck and had a cigarette between his big lips. He slicked back his black hair, exposing the underside of his pale, fat arm. His coon hounds barked like crazy at her as she passed, but he didn't do anything to quiet them. She knew who Ken was, but she didn't know him. Everybody knew who he was--a 240-pound land mine with a tripwire that crossed the length of Skidmore. He looked at everything like he owned it, and mostly he did.

"Hey, girl. You must smell good, you hear them?"

Trena looked back at him and smiled, because that's what you did with that man, and clutched the straps of her backpack tighter.

"I think I smell it, too," he said.

Her face warmed up and she walked faster. With her head down she made sure she only stepped once in each sidewalk block.

"What's your name, little girl?" Ken yelled after her.

She stayed quiet and kept concentrating on the ground beneath her when she noticed that the sun had reached it. She had stepped out from under the trees by accident.

"That's alright, you're shy. I like shy. I'll figure it out, don't you worry," he said.

***

He was always there. His truck on but idling, and the dogs, too. He watched for her, Trena could tell by the way his face went soft when he saw her. She started coming over to him when he called. At first, it made her nervous to get closer, but after a while it was easy, no resistance, only pull.

"That bag looks like it's going to snap you in half," he said.

"It's always this heavy, they give us lots of homework. Mama said high school would be different, I guess she was right."

"You look smart enough to me. I bet you don't need all that, give it here." He reached out of the car and deftly slipped it off her right shoulder. His hand was cold from the beer he had been holding and it felt shocking, like stepping into an ice box. But it was so hot out, that she didn't mind. It happened that easily.

***

Her legs were so skinny on the bench seat of his truck. When she pressed her knees together there was still a gap, a space in which she could fit both her hands.

"I'm not going to bite you, get closer."

And she did, because she didn't want to be rude, but also because of something else she couldn't yet name. A tiny bit of curiosity. She tried to mimic the gap between her thighs with the gap between them, but Ken filled the space. His breath smelled like the warm beer he had in the cup holder in front of them. She had drank some, keeping it in her mouth for a moment so she could feel the bubbles popping on the insides of her cheeks.

"Did you cut your shorts yourself?"

His tongue sounded thick when he talked, and he didn't close his mouth while he held the white strands of thread in his fingers. They parked on one of the busy roads, and people looked in at Trena, only for a second, before they got too scared and quick turned away. It was hot in the car, but he only kept the windows open about an inch as sweat ran down the back of his neck. She kept her hands wrapped around the beer bottle and the label started slipping off in her fingers, or maybe she scratched it off. When she looked down, pieces of it spilled out from under her fingernails.

*****

He was heavy, but not rough. He picked her up from school and when she got in his truck she knew it, this time. He didn't smile at her and he didn't hand her a beer like he usually did. He asked her if she wanted something to eat but she said no, and the rest of it was quiet. He took her to his house. She had never been there before. He had fenced-in areas where his dogs were. A few of them growled and then broke out into howling, while others started snapping their jaws at each other. One dog, a female, lay on the porch panting. Her nipples stretched out long, and Trena didn't want to look. Ken's wife, Alice, hung laundry outside and Trena studied her face as Alice kept her eyes on the shirts in front of her. The clothes were small, kiddie clothes, and a little boy with no shirt came running out with a squirt gun, aiming it at the shirts and spraying.

"Junior, get away from here!" The woman's voice came out sharp and hissing, as she reached for the boy with an arm that looked thin but strong.

The boy smiled while he skidded away from her and ran off to one of the kennels. When the dogs started barking mean at him, Ken snapped his head around.

"Boy, you stay out of there or I'll let them have you!"

Then the small boy paid attention, but he wasn't scared. He sulked away from them and back into the house, throwing the squirt gun on the ground hard enough that a small plastic piece shot up in the air. Ken smiled and kept on walking towards the brown shed near the back of the property.

"Are you on the pill?" He asked as he hooked the lock.

"What for?" Trena thought he was asking if she was sick.

"To keep from getting pregnant."

She shook her head and he shrugged. He took off his belt and told her that she could put her clothes on the chair in the corner. She sat down on a stained mattress on the ground.

"You need to lay back, girl," he said as he climbed on top of her.

The way he positioned himself over her made it so she rose up to him without her meaning to. He still had his socks on and the tops of them rubbed against her toes. She grabbed onto the mattress when he started going and she tried to concentrate on the feel of the springs poking into her back. A stretching started in a place that she had hardly been aware of. She didn't think she had skin on the inside, but she worried that he would tear it. She kept her whole body rigid, she didn't even move her eyes, thinking she needed to keep everything together or else she might break apart. If she held herself, she could keep from dying. Then he stopped moving, and she thought he stopped breathing. His eyes opened wide and staring at something behind her. He was trying to hold together, too, she thought. But that's not what happened. He had let go. Then he crawled back, away from her. She saw a little bit of blood and watched it soak into the mattress between her legs. She had done something wrong, she hadn't kept still enough.

They walked away from the shed, and Alice watched her. Neither of them blinked as they stared into each other. Alice's black hair whipped around her in the wind, sometimes covering her face. She kept her mouth closed, but it felt like she wanted to say something, like her tongue was darting around behind her lips. They watched each other until Trena climbed into the car, and Ken drove her away.

***

Trena didn't know, but Alice did. Alice took her to the doctor for the test. When the doctor asked where Trena's parents were, Alice lied and said she was her mama, but her real mama was too scared to get involved. They were all too scared of Ken. Trena hadn't been home in months. The doctor laughed under his breath and Alice cut him a look like the kind she'd seen Ken cut everyone else.

"She's pregnant," Alice said.

"How do you know?" Ken didn't look up from his cereal, and Trena watched the milk hang off his lip while she stood in the corner. It acted like it was going to fall off back into the bowl, but it stuck to him. She felt sick.

"Look at her, she's been rounding out, you didn't see?"

"Just thought she put on a few, is all."

"Doctor said she's four months. Come summer we'll have another mouth."

"You know I don't like doctors," he said in a low voice.

"Yeah, well, somebody had to tell her."

"She'll make a good mom, I bet," he said.

Alice laughed and went over to the empty sink. She turned the faucet on and ran it. The water came out brown at first, then cleared up. Ken leaned back in his chair and Trena watched him as she put her arms around herself and pressed against the wall. Then he got up fast, knocking the chair over. Alice tried to turn in time to face him, but he was surprisingly quick. He wrapped her black hair around his fist and smashed her face into the wall behind the sink, then he yanked her back so her throat was exposed and she was almost looking at him upside down. Trena had her hands over her ears now, and she couldn't quite hear what he said to her, but when he finished he spit on Alice's face. He let go of her hair and stomped away, grabbing Trena's arm and dragging her with him down the hall.

***

Alice took Trena home to her mom after the baby came and for a few days it was fine. Alice stayed with her and her mom and stepdad and the baby. They slept together at night, on the pullout couch in the basement. In the dark, they clasped each other's hands until they both fell asleep. They woke up that way.

When the baby started to cry, Alice would be the one who got up and brought him to her.

"I don't know what to do with him," Trena said while she cried, still sore from the birth.

"You just make sure he's got food in him and that you love him," Alice said. Trena wondered how she could make sure of that.

Neither of her parents asked what had happened. They didn't talk to them much at all, only to respond when Alice thanked them, which she did over and over, usually holding one of her kids' hands in hers. Trena's parents only nodded. Trena responded to their silence with her own, and tried to only occupy the space her body filled, not letting any of herself spill over. Mostly she stayed in the basement with the dog because it was cool down there, and the only sun that came in came through the small well windows. Alice needed the sun. She went outside, which Trena thought was dangerous. They were supposed to be hiding. They were supposed to keep quiet. Alice couldn't help herself though, she'd go on walks around the block with her kids and come back with the biggest smile on her face, and Trena didn't say anything because she liked the way her face looked like that.

***

Monday, Tuesday, Wednesday, and Thursday things were okay. Then Ken found them and took them back to the farm on Friday. He went back and burned down Trena's parents' house.

When her parents told her what happened, they said the dog had died, too.

"He didn't get out?"

"We found him outside. Ken shot him."

The sheriff brought him in for that. Charged him for the fire and for statutory rape when they saw the birth certificate and found out the baby was his. Ken never denied his own. His lawyer had him out on bail and he waited. The State put Trena and her baby in foster care because her parents were too scared to have her. He waited.

"You belong home. That baby belongs home!" He'd yell out the window of his truck whenever he saw her.

"I love you, baby. I'll marry you, Alice will move out. It'll be just us in there."

She held her breath when he said that. She didn't want Alice to go anywhere, she missed her now.

"Just us," he said.

When she went out the house for doctor visits, he waited. He'd follow her to and from, going real slow in his truck. She walked under trees and listened as the muffler got louder the slower he went. She would try not to run or walk faster, but she would always break and start jogging. The stroller handles would vibrate in her hands and shake her arms all the way up to her teeth until they chattered.

"We always keep the doctor's office a little cooler," the receptionist said.

She sat on the table while the doctor kept his head down and filled out her chart. She had her heels in the stirrups and her legs spread apart, though she worked to keep her knees together while she answered his questions.

"How have you been feeling since the birth?"

"Okay."

"And have you been getting enough sleep?"

"Sure."

"And the baby? Eating alright? Not crying too much."

Billy slept in his stroller, his head no bigger than a softball. His mouth seemed impossibly small. She thought it was strange that the doctor didn't look at the baby as he spoke about him.

"He's fine, I think," she said, keeping her eyes on Billy without blinking.

***

He still waited. He waited over her parents as they signed papers that said he could marry her. After that, the State dropped the rape charges, the arson charges, and even the intimidation charges, which was ironic. He came with the papers to the foster home.

"Should have just given her over in the first place, I wouldn't have bothered you about your own," Ken said to Trena's foster father.

The foster parents didn't touch Trena as she left with him, and they locked the door the moment she stepped outside. Ken walked her to the passenger side first and held the door for her as she climbed in. She reached out for the carrier but he took it with him to his side and put it in between them, leaving a hand on it as he drove.

"We're getting married next week. Need to give this one a proper home," he said as he patted the handle.

"What about Alice?"

"What about her?"

"Where'll she go? And the kids?"

"I'm setting them up at another property, not too far away. She can't live with us anymore."

"How far?"

"How's the little guy been eating? Most of mine have always been little piggies. Tears a woman right up. How's it been for you?" he said, staring at her chest.

"Can we see her, sometimes?"

"I think they've got a cream or something. Should help get them back to normal."

***

It had never been just the two of them before, not since they sat in the truck outside of school. It was quiet and felt so much more treacherous. Trena never wanted Billy to cry so Ken could hear him, so she had him in other rooms. Sometimes, at night, if he was really screaming, she would take him outside and walk away from the house until he stopped. When he stopped, she always turned back. She thought about how it would feel to get into bed with Ken, how his body weighed down the mattress and pulled her towards him. How warm he was.

In the morning, the sheets would be dirty because her blackened feet had tracked in the earth, but Ken didn't care about the dirt. He just told her to clean it later and she would. When he told her to make up the smaller pig for dinner, she did. When he told her to feed the dogs, she did, even though they scared her. When he brought others home, she took Billy and went to the outskirts of the property, never stepping beyond the border, as if something with horribly sharp teeth would kill her on the other side. She learned and she adapted to him. She felt tied down to him.

***

Alice and Trena drank cans of Bud together while their children fought in the front yard of Alice's house. They didn't talk much, mostly they listened to the dogs bark and the kids scream until either one of the women, who hadn't said anything at all, screamed and cursed and threatened. Trena picked at the pimple that rooted deep in the crease of her chin.

"Don't touch it. Only makes it worse," Alice said.

She stopped herself from digging into it with her nails, and instead, she started rubbing it with her finger, almost like a worry stone.

"It'll get infected."

"I thought pimples were only supposed to happen during puberty," Trena said.

"Well, you skipped right through that, so you'll probably have them for the rest of your life."

"I'm serious. I'm 20-years-old and I've never had pimples so big, or so fucking painful."

"Maybe you're pregnant," Alice said, quietly.

"Don't joke."

"The big ones down here." Alice pointed to her chin. "That's hormones. I get one with every monthly, and every one of those." She pointed out to the yard.

Ken came to pick Trena up and neither him nor Alice looked at one another, they never did. When they started rolling down the driveway in his pick-up, he went slow while his children ran up a long side them, and he almost let them reach the road before he peeled out, laughing and honking with a hand out the window. When they drove through town the people scattered into their homes, but lingered just long enough to stare. The look they held in their eyes was the worst sort of pity, like they were saying that that dumb girl doesn't know how bad it is, she can't see it anymore. Lost or gone, it made her feel like a ghost and she hated them. They never looked at Ken. Nobody ever looked at Ken, and she liked that about him.

***

It had been a Jawbreaker. The thing you lick and lick until your tongue becomes raw and bleeds, but you keep going because you can't help it. Her little girl could barely fit the thing in her hand, but she had clung onto it. The Sumy woman and Mrs. Bowenkamp had told Trena that her daughter had taken the thing without paying for it. Said she stole it, or tried to. When her daughter came out with her palms sticky, and blue from the dye, Trena could imagine those handprints on light pink sheets later.

Trena's eyes started to drift as she screamed at the two women. She couldn't see them straight and it only made her angrier.

"She said she didn't take it!" Trena screamed.

"I'm sure it was an accident," Mrs. Bowenkamp said. "But, look there, can't you see her hands?" The woman started to reach towards her daughter and Trena shoved her back.

Trena felt Ken's hand heavy on her shoulder and she went quiet.

"Can I have a pack of camels?" he asked.

"We're all sold out, Sir," Mrs. Bowenkamp said defiantly.

"That's fine, then," Ken said.

When they walked out of the store and climbed into the new Silverado, Trena wanted Ken to ram the truck into their display windows. Instead, he just eyed it, grabbed a cigarette out of the pack with his teeth, and drove away. Trena cried in disappointment.

***

Ken shot Mr. Bowenkamp in the neck with the same rifle he used to put down a sick dog the week before. Trena wished he had killed him, but the old man lived. When Ken was arrested for attempted murder, and taken away in handcuffs, Trena felt proud of him. His lawyer had him out on bail in less than five hours. When he was convicted for the crime, he told her not to worry.

"We'll get them on appeal. I won't see a fucking night in jail, I promise you that. Everything will be fine, just fine," he said.

But she didn't think so. Something had shifted in town. The people no longer looked at her with pity, but outright anger. She felt like she could hear them hissing with their tongues behind their teeth, a big collective sound you don't notice until it suddenly stops. She kept even closer to Ken, and had stopped going over to Alice's, though she made Ken change his will to say if anything happened to both of them, their kids would go live with her. On the night before the appeal, the two of them lay in bed with their chests pressed against each other. Trena studied his eyes, they were wide and watery from not blinking. She kept her hand in his armpit because it was warm and damp. They had the thick blanket up to their shoulders, even though it was 90 degrees in the dark. They didn't sleep or move until morning. He kept her down.

***

She was there with him when he died, and that was something. Just her and him inside that truck. He put the cigarette in his mouth but he didn't light it. He put the keys in the ignition, but he didn't turn it over. He put his hand on the wheel, but he didn't grip it. They were surrounded. She knew most of their faces, but only a handful of their names. She knew they all knew her. That girl. That girl with him. That girl he turned bad. Del came out of his tavern like a Texas ranger in his cowboy hat, leaving the bar unattended. He didn't even lock the door—which made it seem like he'd be right back. He, Mr. Potter, and George Steller had their guns out and pointed.

Trena remembered one of the last times she saw Mr. Potter. He sat at his desk shaking his head at her while she explained why she didn't have her math homework done. She couldn't remember what she said. He must have been retired now, he looked so much older. He might have been the shortest man in Skidmore. He handled his rifle awkwardly, both hands wrapped around the handle with a white-knuckle grip. It was so humid out that she expected the thing to pop out of his hands like a bar of soap. It was close to 100 degrees and every single window on the street was shut. Faces bobbed in and out, all of them peeking behind the curtains. They themselves so close up that their breath fogged up the glass. Trena watched it slowly disappear until they came back and breathed again. All of the kids were out of sight, but she could hear playful screams from somewhere. She looked around and saw them, real little, running around at the top of the hill.

Trena didn't know who shot first, but she knew every gun there went off. It came from behind. The windshield exploded while Trena was being dragged away. Lifted up and out of the passenger seat like she was nothing. The bits of glass sprayed out pink. Then, out of the corner of her eye, she saw Ken slump forward, his head against the steering wheel. Another shot, somewhere to the side, and he went down even further. His skull cracked open and a large piece of it broke the driver's side window. As she screamed and scratched at the air, Mr.

Potter kept asking, who do you want us to get for you, Trena? She was surprised they knew her name. Alice brought her one of her sleeping pills with a glass of water, though Trena wasn't sure why she needed it. She felt like she had been asleep for days, just her eyes had stayed open. A strange new thing she could do.

"Take this," Alice said.

She shoved the pill and water in her face and stood over her while Trena swallowed. Then she sat on the bed, leaning the small of her back against Trena's legs.

"You don't have to go back there, but can you tell me what to get from the house? What you need?"

"Nothing. I don't have anything there."

"What about your clothes, or toiletries."

"Did you see him? Did you see what they did to him?" Trena asked.

"No, I didn't look," Alice said as she laid down next to her, her back a few inches from hers.

"I saw him," Trena said. "I was there with him. I saw him."

"I know, baby."

"I was there," Trena said as she pulled the cover up over her head and closed her eyes so she couldn't see anything but pitch black. The weight of Alice next to her in the bed wasn't enough to pull Trena to her. Soon, she'd float up and no one would be able to stop it.

Ken Rex McElroy terrorized the citizens of Skidmore for his entire adult life. Some of his biggest crimes were committed against the women he claimed, and these women were left helpless to stop him, even within the law, even within their own homes. Finally, when McElroy had shot someone in the neck and looked like he would beat that charge, too, the town took matters into their own hands. McElroy was shot and killed in broad daylight on the street as he sat in his car with his wife, Trena, whom he abused in every sense of the word since she was a child. No one has ever been charged with his murder.

"Nobody wanted to talk to us."
–Retired Missouri State Highway Patrol Trooper Dan Boyer

Chapter Three

Daughters of Fire

Milwaukee, WI. 1883

Oona stared at the red birthmark on her face. It covered most of her right cheek, starting at the soft skin under her eye and reaching down to the corner of her lips with a point. It looked as if something had spilled out of her mouth while she was sleeping and had left a stain. Usually she avoided mirrors, but she wasn't quite used to the Newhall House and had snuck up on herself. She put a hand up to her face instinctively, not to cover it, but to trace the borders. It was a habit. She liked feeling the subtle line where her two different skins met. She noticed her hand was turning red to match, and seemingly permanently pruned. Oona was lucky enough, her mother had told her before she left Ireland, to be given a job in a nice hotel in America—possible through a relative, some cousin of her mother's that Oona still had not met. She wondered if her mother knew how much colder it would be. Oona had not packed properly, though her mother reminded her to bring everything. There were things she left behind in secret, in case. Her good stockings, for instance.

She was supposed to be a maid, doing turndown service and assisting the guests, but the manager stuck her back in the laundry room after he saw her face. She was out, today, because all the girls had to be. Someone important would be arriving soon and the staff was frenzied.

"Can you help me with these curtains?" Minnie appeared behind her in the mirror, pressing dark red velvet against her back. Oona turned around and gathered it up in her arms. She shared a bed with Minnie in a small room on the sixth floor with the rest of the maids. She had told Oona that the mark on her face looked a little like a heart, and that was something Oona's mother had told her once, but only once.

"Do you know who's coming?" Oona asked.

"No, but it must be somebody special, I've never had to move the paintings from the hallways in here before."

Oona surveyed the room and felt claustrophobic; the walls almost completely covered with paintings, posters, and mirrors in different shapes reflecting segmented parts of people rushing in around in front of them; ankles, waists, knees just hanging in midair. Oona and Minnie dropped the curtains into the wash bin and brought out bright green ones to hang, then they started to scrub the wood floors, turning their dresses black at the knees. Every time the door opened, enough of the cold would get in so Oona could see the breath coming out of her mouth.

They finished close to breakfast time and Oona went back to the kitchen to help with the washing while Minnie set the tables in the dining room. Oona liked to watch her do this from the little window in the door because every so often Minnie would pick up a spoon, or fork, and slip it in her apron pocket. There didn't seem to be a reason why Minnie would pick one piece of silver over another, and her face changed over when she did it; she became almost other worldly beautiful as she dropped her eyelids down and looked around the room without trying to move her face. She only ever took one at a time, and Oona guessed this was so they wouldn't crash together in her pockets, but once they were taken Oona never saw them again. She imagined Minnie swallowing them like a fire eater who puts flaming sticks down his throat. Her stomach full of silver.

The house mistress, Miss Angie, came into the dining room as Minnie's hand was slipping back out of her apron. Oona hadn't even seen what she took. Miss Angie came back to the kitchen and opened the door.

"Do you all want to come out to the front of the house and see them?"

"See who, Miss Angie?" Minnie asked from behind her.

"Our guests."

"But who are they?"

"Well, let's go take a look, no?"

Oona came out of the kitchen first, but only to get out of the way of the others coming quickly behind her. She watched them crowd one another down the hall when Minnie grabbed her hand and pulled her along.

There was a crowd. Guests had come down from their rooms dressed as if they were going out for the evening. Finally, the doors swung open and a gust of frigid air blew in. Applause erupted, but she couldn't see anything.

"Dear God," cried Minnie. "That's General Tom Thumb and his wife!"

Oona had never seen a dwarf before, but two of them strode in front of her smiling and shaking hands. Minnie was holding Oona's hand with a grip that was stronger than Oona expected. Her untrimmed nails were digging into her palm, but Oona was too afraid to stop her as the pain was the only thing keeping her in place. Oona had never thought of a person's height as something that would scare her, but when she saw them standing no higher than a tabletop, she wanted to run outside. The crowd had pressed in on them, forcing her forward, all of them buzzing at the same pitch.

"Look at them," Minnie whispered sharply to her. "They look like they're playing grown-ups."

Oona was too afraid to look, at first, so she kept her eyes down, watching people's

feet as they tried to get closer. Their shoes were dirty from the black snow outside, and Oona's skirt soaked up the puddle forming on the wood floor. Minnie kept bobbing up and down on her toes to get a better look. The bartender brought over a stool, holding it high above his head as he walked it through the crowd.

"Here you go, General," the bartender shouted.

Minnie tried to move them forward, interjecting her small bony body into the crowd, yanking hard on Oona's arm, but she stayed put.

"What's wrong with you? I want to see," Minnie said.

Oona couldn't make herself move. She felt like she'd be going closer to the edge of a very high cliff.

"Do you need me to help you, sir?" the bartender asked the General.

"Not me, no. But if you could assist my wife."

The couple got up on the stools, and Minnie stopped dragging her.

Oona thought it wouldn't be so bad if she looked then, and she lifted her head up. The General was tired; that was plain on his face. The bags under his eyes sagged into two prominent U's, and a beard covered up his chin, but not the fat around his neck. Both he and his wife dressed well. She wore a dark silky, green gown that bustled in the back, with lace trimming along the bodice and sleeves. She was beautiful. Her dark brown hair matched her eyes, and for however old the General appeared, nobody would have been able to guess his wife's age other than to say she was youthful. Oona was suddenly jealous. The General watched his wife, too, in between handshakes and smiles. The smile he reserved for her was subtler than the over drawn grin he had for the guests.

"They used to have an act where the world's tallest man would balance them both, one standing in each hand," Minnie said.

"You've seen them before?"

"I never did in person, I just heard about it when my mother would take me to the theater. They had posters up near where we bought tickets, drawings of the two of them kissing over the Tall Man's head. She won't believe this."

"I've never been to a theater."

"You say 'The Theater.' Mother used to be an actress. She liked to go back and watch the plays she knew. She loved it there. Said she could even see them with her eyes closed."

Oona closed her eyes and tried to see something she knew, but only saw the hem of her skirt getting ruined when she felt it, wet, on her foot.

"I wonder where their baby is, they used to bring it around in a cigar box as a cradle."

"What?"

Minnie made her fingers into a square, "That's what mother told me. She said I had the same cheeks when I was small. Naturally rouged."

Oona's face itched.

***

Minnie made her stay up late. The girls hid in the stairwell off of the dining room where they could see the General and his wife. They ate dinner alone but were frequently bothered by guests stopping at their table. He had two drinks, while she had more. He eyed her when she ordered the fifth one, but she didn't look back. She had the lamb, and he had a stuffed steak with mushrooms, which she warned him about getting.

"You'll be up all night bloated if you eat that," his wife said.

"I'll be up all night anyway, so damn cold in our room."

Suddenly, Minnie turned around. There was a hand on her shoulder, and in the other hand was a small silver fork. Miss Angie, the house mistress, held it in front of Minnie's face.

"Do you know how this ended up in your apron, Minnie?" Miss Angie's face was like stone, setting the lines deep around her mouth, making her skin look like dried clay under the make-up. She smiled at her girls so often that she could have been a stranger just then.

Minnie was silent for a long time before weakly saying, "I don't know." Oona kept her eyes squarely on her shoes, studying every scuff mark she could find. There were many.

"I found more in your mattress."

How could Oona not have felt them?

"Minnie, I can't keep you."

"Miss Angie, I'll give them back, they're all still there." Minnie pleaded, her hands clutching together, pressing her knuckles in.

"I'm sorry, dear. You can stay the night, but you'll have to leave in the morning."

"You can't. I don't know where to go."

Miss Angie got up and climbed the stairs as Minnie watched, stuttering out the start of a word but not being able to say it. Oona's chest was warm, and she wanted to leave the stairway—she felt too close to everything. Minnie turned back and stared at the ground for a long time. Oona thought to put a hand on her, but didn't.

There was a loud scratch against the floor in the dining room as General Tom Thumb pushed out from the table. He helped his wife out of her seat and the two of them walked arm in arm towards the elevator.

Minnie shot up, "Come on," she said, grabbing Oona's hand.

"I've got extra blankets in my room, General," Minnie said loudly once they caught up to them.

An uncomfortable warmth spread quickly from Oona's chest to her face, and she put her hands over her cheeks. The General and his wife leaned away as Minnie stopped abruptly before them.

"I could bring them down for you if you'd like me to," Minnie said.

The General's wife kept her eyes on her husband, as he wearily smiled. Oona prayed for the car to come down.

"I'm sure we'll be fine, dear, but that is kind of you," he said, trying to keep his face composed.

"Can I ask how your baby is?" Minnie asked.

"What?" he asked.

"I'm sorry, it must be grown now."

"Minnie, we should leave them be," Oona said.

"My mother used to point at the posters and tell me I looked just like that when I was baby," Minnie said.

"We don't have any children," the General said, trying, still, to keep the smile.

Oona wrapped her arms around herself to be as small as possible.

"Sorry? Have they gone? We lost my sister when she was only four-years-old, she caught the flu and couldn't survive it. I had it, too, but I got better. I'm terribly sorry for your loss. From the pictures it looked very happy."

Oona had wrapped her hand around Minnie's wrist and pressing down on the middle underneath as hard as she could. But Minnie didn't notice.

"We should go now," Oona said between her teeth.

"That wasn't ours," the General's wife said.

"Lavinia," the General said.

"It's fine, Tom. We're not working anymore; it doesn't matter."

"If you want to keep coming to these places and being treated like this, it matters," the General said.

"Treated like what? Like dolls to be played with? We're too old now," she said. "And it is damn cold."

"Whose baby was it?" Minnie asked.

Tom turned to Oona, and she thought he might say something, but he only glanced at her birthmark before turning away. Oona quickly put her hand up against it, but then forced herself to drop it back down by her side, feeling the pull of her mother's hand on hers the way she had done before when Oona would try to hide it.

"Which one? It was a different baby with every town. It was always a baby, too. They didn't want a child growing bigger than either of us."

"It's time for bed, Lavinia," the General said, pulling her away from them. Oona thought Minnie might follow, but she only watched. Minnie stood still until Oona gently grabbed two of her fingers.

"Come on. It's late. We should go up before Miss Angie checks the room."

***

Minnie walked as if she were a wheeled toy Oona dragged by a string; coming along easily behind her, but wooden. The sconces lining the halls were turned down and cast an orange shadow suggesting a warmth that wasn't there. They walked up the stairs to the sixth floor, and Oona slowly opened the door to their room. They tried not to wake the six other girls as they crept between the beds in the dark. They both unbuttoned their dresses and stepped out of them without saying a word. The cold went through Oona's shift like an intruder, and she quickly got underneath the blankets, though they weren't much warmer. She waited for Minnie to get in as she shivered, but Minnie continued to quietly cry next to the bed.

"Come to bed, Minnie. You'll feel better after you rest."

As she waited, Oona listened to the other girls in the room as they slept. They had seemed to synchronize their breathing, and Oona wanted nothing more than to join them. She pressed her teeth together as Minnie started swaying back and forth. She needed her body heat to keep warm enough to sleep; she couldn't even close her eyes while Minnie stood there, so awfully out of place. She tugged on Minnie's shift and she sat down, wiping her eyes before getting underneath the covers. The two of them pushed their backs together as they curled into outward facing crescents.

"How come you never said anything?" Minnie asked, her voice sounding remote—it could have come from any place in the room, even the ceiling.

"About what?"

"I know you saw me do it."

Oona tried to think of how to answer this without sounding like a deviant. *I watched because I liked to.*

"I didn't want to shame you."

"I didn't feel shame."

"Oh."

Minnie laughed, a strange single laugh that came out of the back of her throat, "it made me feel good's why I did it. It made everything inside go smooth, instead of how it's always twisted up. Did you mother ever pet your hair, like you were a cat?"

"No."

"Do you think my mother knew about the baby?" Minnie asked.

She had asked it so quietly, but Oona was sure she woke the room. Neither of them moved for a moment. Oona thought about her own mother, and it made her ache. Did she know about this place? How cold it would be?

"I don't know what she knew, but sometimes people will play along for you, and to keep from having to answer any questions, you see?"

"I think, maybe, she didn't know. Or else she wouldn't have said. She always said she couldn't lie for anything."

"Wasn't she an actress?"

As the intonation of her voice rose up, Oona had an urge to put her hand over her mouth to stop the words coming out of it. Instead, she kept her hands in between her thighs and ducked her head, so her chin pressed against her chest. She waited for Minnie to say something, but nothing came.

***

Oona couldn't tell for how much longer Minnie had cried, but she knew she was finally asleep when her breathing matched the chorus in the room. She could smell the salt of Minnie's skin, and it was strong enough to keep her awake. It wasn't fair. Minnie was sweating terribly. She often soaked the bed through to the mattress, and Oona wondered if this was due to how much she moved during her waking hours, or if it was her lack of ability to hold anything inside of her. Oona was pushed to the very edge of the bed and braced herself for the cold dampness that would eventually reach her. It reminded her of falling asleep on the boat. She would close her eyes thinking she would feel water lapping at her skin at any moment. Her mother loved the water, and would tell her children that she must have been born a seal but learned to walk on land before she could remember. Oona wondered if the patch on her face was her seal parts, given to her by her mother, but Oona hated the water.

Minnie jerked and let out a deep sigh. The sound of the sigh continued for a long time, and Oona wondered how a person could have so much air in them until she realized the sound was not coming from Minnie, but outside the door. She sat up in bed and looked at the slit of light coming from the hallway.

"What's that?" another girl asked from her bed.

"Don't know. Could be a pipe burst," Oona said without taking her eyes off the light.

Then she heard heavy footsteps coming down the hall. Not quite running, but they were urgent. Not like the drunks stumbling back to their room at night.

"Who's that, then?" the girl asked.

"How should I know?"

"Is something burning?" another girl asked.

Oona got out of bed and walked over to the door. She put her ear against it, but heard nothing except the wind, like someone had opened all of the windows, which didn't make any sense. She thought about opening the door to see, but as she wrapped her hand around the handle, another pair of footsteps came harder than the first, and she snatched her hand away. Now all the girls were sitting up in their beds, except Minnie, but Oona could tell she was awake.

Oona turned back towards the door and took a deep breath. Something was burnt somewhere. She opened the door and went out into the hallway. Miss Angie was already coming toward her in her nightgown and no slippers. It occurred to Oona that she had never seen a stranger's bare feet in the light, before. It was the bare feet, not the light smoke filling the hallway, that scared her.

"Come on, let's go back in your room, Oona. You can't get out down the stairs, and the elevator isn't working."

"What's happened?"

But Miss Angie shook her head and herded her back in where all the girls were gathered together, except Minnie still, who was folded into herself on the bed, with her eyes like glass balls reflecting the light from the hallway.

"What's the matter?" Minnie asked.

"Nothing, girls. We just have to wait for someone to come get us," Miss Angie said, hurriedly closing the door. Oona thought, how would they find us with the door shut? How would they know which door was ours?

"Get us, why? What's happening?" one of the girls asked.

The smell of smoke grew stronger. Oona could taste it in the back of her throat, and a sound like a high wind became louder.

"I don't know, dear. Can't say for sure," Miss Angie said. "Maybe we'll open a window, though, and get some fresh air in."

"It's freezing," Minnie said. "We shouldn't do that."

"It'll be best if we do—will someone help me do it?"

Miss Angie ran across the room and two of the girls joined her at the window.

"Miss Angie," Oona said, pointing down at the smoke coming underneath the door.

Miss Angie turned with wide eyes, not saying a thing as she watched it curl in. A panic gripped Oona and she opened the door to the hallway. She couldn't see anything beyond the thick gray smoke, anymore. A warm glow accompanied by a wicked heat forced her back into the room. The sound came from the heat, somehow. She slammed the door and grabbed a blanket from the bed, falling to her knees to stuff it underneath. The heat got into her mouth and seized her throat like someone wrapping a strong hand around it. The smoke surrounded her tongue as if she had swallowed coal. Oona leaned back on her heels to see if it had worked, if the smoke had stopped, and while it had slowed, it was still getting in along the seams in the doorframe.

"What should we do? Was there anybody out there?" a girl asked.

Oona kept her back to the room as she shook her head. One of them started to cry.

"Let's get closer to the window, ladies. Come on," Miss Angie said.

Oona crawled over to the group, and Minnie came beside her. They held each other's hands as the room grew warmer.

"Shouldn't somebody say something? Shouldn't we pray?" one of the girls asked.

"That's a good idea," Miss Angie said. "Let's all say the Hail Mary while we wait."

So they prayed, while the smoke came in, repeating it until Miss Angie fell over on the floor. One of the girls screamed at this, while more started to cry. Oona noticed Minnie start to breathe heavily, skipping words during the prayer.

"Hail Mary . . . blessed . . . mother."

The room was almost filled with smoke and the girls sucked at the air from the window like fish coming to the surface of a pond. Minnie loosened her hold on Oona's hand, and then suddenly it was no longer there at all.

"Minnie?" she asked.

"We're not going to get out of here," Minnie said.

There was a collective moment of desperation from the girls, as if Oona could see their resolve evaporating.

"I want . . ." Minnie paused, then she struggled to her feet, trying to breathe but only coughing.

"I want my mother to have a body to bury," she yelled over the noise that had become almost deafening.

The girls parted as she put a foot up on the window ledge and then her other. She held on for a moment before letting herself go. Oona was not closest to the window, so she did not see her fall; she only saw her disappear from view. The same girl who screamed when Miss Angie fainted, screamed again before passing out herself. Then, none of them spoke. None of them prayed, not even silently to themselves. They closed their eyes because having them open was too painful. They put their foreheads on the ground, not in a plea, but in an effort to breathe. Oona was the only one who kept her head up. She kept opening her eyes to look at the window, wondering when she would do it. How much longer would she wait? She thought she could still smell the salt from Minnie's skin. The room was hot enough now that it felt like nails were scratching inside her throat when she breathed. She wished she had held tighter to Minnie's hand if only Minnie could have dragged her along.

She could not keep her eyes open any longer and finally bowed her own head to the floor. In her dark, she heard her own mother's voice, repeating the way Miss Angie had said, "I can't keep you, I can't keep you." Oona tried to reply, but her throat burned. She wanted to open her eyes and find her, but the smoke was too thick. She reached out and felt nothing. She had expected that. "I can't keep you," she heard again, but as loud as if her mother had said it in her ear.

Oona came to six stories high over Broadway St. Someone had her tight around her thighs and hung over their shoulder, and they moved slowly away from the window. The ladder worked as a bridge between the Newhall House and the neighboring building. Its rungs shook with each step the fireman took. Oona's arms swung wildly as she could get hold of nothing but air. Flames shot out of the windows, and darted around like long, vicious tongues, wagging hungrily. She tried to adjust her eyes and see beyond them. Below were dozens of faces all with different expressions; shock and horror. Some were plain and some were smiling in odd, restrained ways. Smoke came from their mouths and they rubbed their hands together to warm them. Minnie had fallen somewhere down there, some-where close to where the fire watchers were with their eyes wide. Oona tried to find her, but she could only see the faces, and then she couldn't bare to keep her eyes open.

***

Oona's clothes still smelled days after the fire, even though the nurses at the hospital had given her new ones. She would sometimes forget about the smell, or get used to it, and then suddenly get a strong whiff. She would search for the source of the smell, lifting her collar and sniffing her armpits, as if she had absorbed it and was now producing it as her own odor. The nurses thought the mark on her face was a burn, and it was covered in ointment. She didn't mind letting them think that. A scar was better than a stain from birth. She had her own bed for the first time in her life. A nun who had visited the girls in the hospital asked them all if they could write to someone on their behalf.

"Just to tell them you're alive."

"I'm not sure where my mother is, right now. She's an actress, you see. She travels," Oona said.

The nurse handed her a newspaper that said General Tom Thumb and his wife had also been on the sixth floor, barely escaping if not for the fireman that carried them out the same way they had carried out the girls, over his shoulders on a ladder above Broadway. There was a drawing of them both tucked neatly under one strong arm. But that wasn't true, they had been on the second floor. Oona had watched them walk up the stairs and turn down the hallway. She wondered if Minnie had seen them then, too. Or, if maybe she had seen them cross from where she lay, even with her eyes closed. Mrs. Thumb told the paper that she felt sorry.

"I'm so thankful that we made it out alive, but I can't help myself from thinking about those young girls who perished. As a mother, my heart breaks for them. For them and their mothers."

The Newhall House Hotel was less than 30 years old but had built up a reputation for fires in Milwaukee. It was also a popular spot for celebrities to stay when visiting. The service workers, almost entirely female, stayed on the 6th floor–many being Irish immigrants including my own several times great grandmother. On the winter night of the final fire, the flames raced up the elevator shafts making escape nearly impossible. As the Irish maids on the 6th floor prayed for rescue or mercy, some jumped rather than burn. Just when all hope seemed lost, a ladder came across from the neighboring building, and the firefighters carried out the remaining women from the 6th floor. The word that was passed down through my family's telling of this story was desperation. A moment of pure desperation led a girl to throw herself out the window so her parents would have a body to bury. But if she had only waited, just a little longer, she would have been saved. My family kept this desperate girl in their stories for over a century, and I'm not sure if that is a mercy or a disgrace.

"This place is going to be gone if we don't get some help!"
–Watchman William McKenzie

Chapter Four

Maneater

Manhattan, NY. 1916

E sther knew that all good stories had blood and teeth. She knew this even though she was young. This was why her father loved the shark stories, and why her brother Roy listened. Her father read them out loud while they ate.

"Really? At the table?" She said because she thought this was something her mother might've said—though she hadn't heard her own mother say anything, she heard other mothers say things like this.

"It swam down this creek here and ate that little boy." His finger traced the line until it hit the X. Her father put the paper down on the table, got up and walked quickly over to the kitchen sink. Then, he started going heel to toe across the floor, into the hallway, and all the way to the front door.

"The creek is just a few feet wider than our apartment, I think," he said, with a clever smile on his face.

Just then, their home felt smaller—dangerously claustrophobic. Esther took a deep breath. Her father came back and sat down heavily. He picked the paper back up and held it close to his face.

"*The poor boy's leg was left in ribbons, from knee to ankle,*" he read.

"Right here." Roy kicked at her leg, but Esther was quick and he missed, hitting her chair instead. She kept her face down, away from her brother, but she knew he was white mad. She knew he was wide eyed and chewing on his lips so the color blanched out of them.

There wasn't a time that Esther could remember where she wasn't watching her brother out of the corner of her eye. He was sneaky and quick with violence, pinching the underside of her arms or behind her knees, marking up the soft fleshy parts of her that no one would notice. But then, as he got older, he became careless and his transgressions were done in plain sight, evidence left in front of everyone to see, like a cat bringing home a dead bird and dropping it at your feet. A very bloody gift. The harder their father went at him, the more showy Roy got.

"What do you know about that? Says they'll pay $100 to whoever catches the monster."

"I bet I could catch him," Roy said.

"Yeah? With what, your hands? You ever been on a boat before? You know how to swim?" Their father said.

"Well, do you?" Roy said.

"Why don't you go ahead and try, this thing has already eaten four people—why don't you see if you can make it five and make all our lives a little easier," their father said.

***

That night Esther slept in rows and rows of teeth. She couldn't see anything in her dreams, there was just the dark, and a gnashing sound. But she knew they were teeth—she could feel them with her hands. Everywhere she touched would be a sharp, triangle, serrated point piercing into her skin. The first night she had the dream, she woke up screaming and her brother, Roy, pinned her to the bed with a pillow over her face. Their room was small, and their small beds only had a very small space between them, and Roy bridged the gap without even touching the ground. She never heard him coming. He did this until she thrashed underneath him, kneeing the middle of his back. He let go and she gasped for air, not being able to control how loud the sound came out of her mouth. Their father came in, a sudden giant in the dark, and grabbed Roy by the hair, pulling him to the ground. Roy clawed at his father's grip while Esther stared at him, filled with both vindication and an unwanted pity. She could smell the salt from his skin.

"Are you done? Because I can keep going until you stop moving for good."

Roy nodded his head as best as he could without pulling against their father's fist. Their father let go, wiping strands of hair off on his chest before leaving. Roy crawled back into bed, and with his back turned toward her he said, "If you make another noise, I'll kill you." He sounded the way she thought a snake would sound.

***

The next morning, Roy came in with the paper and a big smile on his face that made Esther feel sick.

"They got the fish."

"What do you mean?" Their father said, and it was unusual to hear them talk together in the same excited pitch. Their eyes opening wide in response to each other's. It was a receive and response.

"Here, see?"

The first thing Esther saw was the mouth, and only the mouth. It was exactly as she had dreamt it. A black hole that she knew went on forever, covered in teeth and the ribbons of a little boy's skin. Gnashing for always. The whole world would have fallen in, eventually. She wasn't certain that it still wouldn't. She could feel a slight pull in the center of her stomach. She couldn't understand the rest of it. She didn't know where its parts were, or what they were. She couldn't tell if it had eyes or arms or what else. But she knew it had a mouth.

"Says it's going to be on display on Sunday. In the window of that paper. Can we go see it?"

In the picture, four heads peeked over the top of the thing. You couldn't see half of their faces, but you could tell by their eyes that they were smiling. Squeezing themselves together like friends behind the monster in front of them. They didn't even look proud, just happy. She tried to picture her father there, looking that way, but she couldn't place him. He wouldn't fit.

Roy was staring at their father and smiling—waiting for an answer. Esther could see a hole forming in the back of his mouth. A tooth was going bad, bad enough that you'd look away if he caught you staring at it.

***

Once, after a particularly bad and early bout with Roy, when Esther would still ask what she did wrong that made her brother so mean, their father turned his back on her. While she cried in the kitchen chair holding a wet rag on her cheek, he told her.

"He misses his mother."

This wasn't an answer. Esther kept crying and said, "I miss her, too."

"No. No you don't, sweetheart. You can't miss what you didn't know. That boy loved his mother. God help me, he needs his mother."

And after that, Esther stopped herself from missing her mom. She couldn't grow that same meanness inside of her.

***

People came out of church and went down to Harlem to stand in line. Esther felt underdressed. As the three of them stood there, she found five stains on her clothes. She didn't know what to do with stains. What exactly you needed to mix in order to get rid of them. Whenever she asked her father, he told her he didn't see them.

"Can I go over there?" Roy pointed to the group of kids playing *come with me*. He had been jumping in his skin ever since they started standing still. He never waited well.

"Go 'head," their father said, just as happy to get rid of him.

Roy left them both in his wake, his arms and legs jutting out at harsh angles as he ran off.

"Find me before you get to the fish."

"Yeah," their father said.

Esther let out a breath she didn't know she'd been holding, and prepared to settle into the familiar silence with her father. Somehow the line moved, though she didn't feel like she was moving. They turned the corner from Hart St. to 125th, and suddenly people were celebrating. The street was crowded with games and food stands and people selling all kinds of things. Right at the corner, a man stood behind a small wooden table with lots of little glass bowls. His face was all screwed up as he tried to keep the sun out. His lips were drawn up over his teeth, showing several holes. Then his eyes found Esther, and she felt like she got caught in something.

"How'd you like a baby golden shark, dear?"

She grabbed onto her father's arm. Inside each of the bowls was a small orange fish, swimming so slowly she wondered if they were real. Then one of them turned and swam to the other side of their bowl, knocking itself headfirst into the glass.

"Why don't you ask your dad to get you one. It'll grow up real big."

She pressed her cheek to her father's coat, inhaling the smell he carried with him from work. She didn't know what it was, not exactly, but it smelled like rocks and soap and something else that could sting you.

"How much?" her father asked the man whose smile now seemed impossibly big.

"Just five cents. One nickel to take home a friend of the Terror of the Century."

"What do you think, Essie? You'll take care of him? Make sure he gets strong." Her father wasn't looking at her as he reached under his hat for the change, so he didn't see the fear on her face. He took one step out of line, then quickly moved back.

"Don't want to lose our spot here, can you bring one over?"

"Sure, I can."

The man started peering into the bowls, one by one, his face up close, his nose over the opening.

"This's the one for you, right here." He came over, and Esther could smell him now—like fish and garbage. He was dirty. His face shined from grease and sweat, and he walked like he might fall down. Her father put his arms up to catch him, but he waved them away.

"S'alright. I'm just missing a few toes on my right foot." Then he looked at Esther and winked. "left my feet dangling in the water a little too long, didn't I?"

He handed Esther the bowl and took the money. "See how it shines in the sun, like that?"

Esther had been too afraid to look at the fish, but out of the corner of her eye she saw something flash. The fish sparkled.

***

Her father talked to strangers that looked like him--men with dirt on their clothes who sounded just the same. Whatever they were saying floated past Esther as an imperceptible hum. She wouldn't have been able to decipher between words if she tried. She held the fishbowl tight from the bottom, wondering if it had any teeth yet, or if it had just one sharp, tiny triangle sticking from the top of its mouth. She thought about what she would feed it. Small bites of her dinner from the tip of her finger. She would need to teach it to be gentle with her. To come when she called it. To behave.

"My God," said another voice ahead of her. A woman's voice. The light way she spoke made it sound as if she were talking to Esther directly--whispering something sad to her. When Esther looked to see who it was, she only saw shoulders and backs. People were pressing closer together, all of them bunching up, and then she realized they were near the monster.

Esther stopped dead on the sidewalk and held her breath. She realized she didn't want to see it. She didn't want to see the thing that ate up children in the creek. She didn't want to stare into the hole that swallowed smiling bathers on holiday. She felt her father's hand take hold of her shoulder and squeeze.

"Almost there, Es," he said, and he pushed her forward. She felt sick—she thought about Roy's knees and elbows as he ran off, wishing, for possibly the first time ever, that she had gone with him.

Her father maneuvered her through the last few people in front of them, squeezing her between a woman's hip and the back of a man's hand, his knuckles scrapping against her cheek.

The shark hung in the window, swaying almost leisurely behind the glass. Esther's face reflected over its gills. The leather skin folded at the corners of the mouth, which had been propped open by a sanded down branch. She stabbed at the roof of her own mouth her tongue, trying to create the sensation of a stick in her mouth. Next to the shark, displayed out in small pieces like splinters of wood, were bones. A sign next to them read: Young Female Great White Shark, 350 lbs, 7 ½ feet long. Shin Bone of Young Boy Found in STOMACH.

"And that thing," her father said into her ear as he pointed, "just hiding all the time down there. Waiting."

"Daddy," she said.

"Mmhmm?"

"Can we go home?"

"Yeah. Let's get Roy."

***

They found him alone, scratching at dirt on the ground with his fingers, trying to pry something out from between the cracks in the sidewalk. His shoulders hunched when their father called him, but he didn't turn around. He wanted whatever it was, bad.

"Roy, get up, let's go," their father said. His voice was low, like he was daring Roy to raise it.

"There's an Indian Head Nickel here, dad."

"Yeah? How do you know?"

"I saw some boy drop it."

"He's probably going to come back looking for it, and I don't feel like dancing with some kid's father. Come on, let's go."

"What about the shark?"

"Seen it already."

"But you were supposed to come get me."

"Tried to find you," their father lied.

"I've been here the whole time. Even after all the other kids left, I waited just right here."

"You must have moved without knowing."

"I swear I didn't," Roy stretched his neck out in indignation.

"Leave it be. Time to go."

"Then let me get this nickel, I can go back later."

"Roy."

"But I almost got it," he said, grunting between words.

"Won't ask again."

Roy let out a frustrated scream and slapped the pavement with his dirty hand.

"Calm down."

Roy stomped over, brushing his hands off on his pants. When he saw the fish in Esther's hands he stopped walking.

"What's that she's got?"

Esther gripped the bowl tighter, turning away from her brother so he might not see it. The look on her father's face made her nervous—because he was nervous, but then he straightened.

"Man gave it to us over there."

"Gave it to you?"

"Said your sister was pretty enough not to pay." Their father patted her head as if she were a house pet.

"She's not pretty."

"Well, she's got a fish, doesn't she?"

"If I can pull out that Nickel, I can get one myself."

"That's enough. It's time to go home. You've both got school tomorrow." He grabbed Roy by the back of the neck and shoved him, almost making him fall, but Roy caught himself, sucking air between his teeth as he straightened. He shot a look at Esther, and she knew she was in trouble.

***

She wanted to hide her fish somewhere. She thought about tearing up a floorboard under her bed and making a home for it. She'd put little things down there—thimbles, change, needles; shiny objects that might make it not miss the world so terribly. Or, at least, distract it for a little while. It might not grow so big in the dark, but that would be okay. She would make sure it ate what it was supposed to eat—sleep when it was supposed to sleep. She felt the floor with her toes for any loose pieces, but found nothing promising. She knew she couldn't keep it out in the room with her and Roy. It would make things worse. She kept it on the ground on her side of the room between her bed and the wall. Her father had asked her to share it with her brother. He said it without looking at her--shameful with his eyes on his knees.

"No," she said, for the first time.

He sighed then he nodded. "Okay."

Her father was more than nervous.

At night, she'd wake from her teeth dreams and search for her fish with her hands, being careful to not knock the bowl over, but just feel for it. She'd find the opening and stick a finger in—sometimes brushing against its scales and sometimes dangling it so the fish might come to her. One morning she woke with her finger still in the bowl, the fish swimming around it as if it were chasing its tail, and her brother staring at her from the doorway standing completely still—she didn't even think he was breathing.

***

It was dark when she woke, but she could tell it was almost morning. She could hear something. Birds, she thought, at first. But then it sounded different as she came out of her sleep. She could hear better. The sound of something hitting against glass. She couldn't see in the dark, but she could picture Roy in the doorway, warning her of whatever was going to happen next. Out of habit, like the way she used to twirl her hair when she got scared, she put her finger in the bowl, but the fish did not come. She wormed it around until she felt something that hadn't been there before. A long hard thing. She grabbed and pulled it free from the gravel she had found on the street and put in the bowl.

Her eyes, adjusting now, saw the golden jewel she loved stabbed through with a fork—all four prongs piercing its skin. Each second her eyes could see better in the dark and she could see what her brother had done. Despite all his training of her, she screamed. Without letting go of the fork, she screamed. She could hear him wrestle out of bed, falling to the floor tangled up in his sheets. Then she heard the heavier sound of her father's feet hitting the ground. He came in and grabbed Roy before he could reach her mouth, which was swallowing up the world. Her father threw him against the wall and began yelling something at him she couldn't understand, she couldn't quite hear. All she could hear was the gnashing sound of her teeth. All she could think about was what they would find in her stomach if she could grow big and live forever in the dark.

Swimmers were snatched by man-eating sharks off the Jersey Shore in the middle of the summer holiday in 1916. Until then, Sharks weren't considered a danger. After, everything changed. The 1916 New Jersey Shark Attacks sparked a mass panic that has endured for over a century. Without them, we wouldn't have Jaws, or fears of the things we can't see underneath us in dark waters.

"The one purpose in which everybody shares," the Times *Reported, "is to get the shark, to kill it, and to see its body drawn up on the shore, where all may look and be assured it will destroy no more."*
–Close to Shore, The New Jersey Shark Attacks

Chapter Five

She Goes First

New York City, NY. 1928

Lula couldn't remember when Tom started discreetly coming to and leaving their bed, but there must have been a particular day when he decided to be quieter. It didn't matter, she was such a light sleeper that it wasn't the bird or the phone call that woke her, it was the air at her back, his absence. When she came into the kitchen, he was moving very fast, almost so her tired eyes couldn't keep up with him, and he blurred as he paced from one spot to another. Lula pulled her hair behind her ears and watched him. It had been a long time since she had seen him like this, and she was nervous.

"Who was on the phone?"

"Work, they want me for something big up in New York," he said over his shoulder.

"New York? Why?"

A few months ago, they had moved into their DC apartment from his studio in Chicago. Tom had said it was too cramped for him there, and there was an opening at the DC bureau of the Chicago Tribune. But Lula didn't think it was any bigger, now. Just emptier. The only furniture being the bed, a couch in the living room, and a kitchen table set that came cheap because it had been scratched in the store.

"You know that big case where the woman killed her husband? The dumbbell murder?"

Lula shook her head, she didn't pay attention to the news, which Tom had liked at the start. She knew it made him feel good to tell her about things.

"They're executing them next week and they want me to come in and take pictures."

"Pictures of what?"

"The execution," he said with a too big smile. "Just her, though. They're going to run it on the front page."

"You can't be serious," she said. "You mean, when she dies?"

"Mmhmm."

"Why would anyone want to see that?" Lula asked while letting her vision blur as she stared out the window. The snow was coming down in big heavy flakes as a few men in dark jackets started to make their trek to work.

"People can't not look," he said.

He would be working for the *New York Daily News*, he explained, because no photographers were being let into Ruth Snyder's execution, just reporters. The editors thought it would be clever to bring someone in that the guards had never seen before. They hired another man to make them a camera special for the job. The body of it would be strapped to Tom's ankle, the lens facing out and angled up, and the shutter release would be wired up through his pant leg to the arm of his jacket, so he could press it as if he were clicking a pen. It was single use.

She turned to look at Tom. His face was always astonishing. Hard set features, nothing soft there, not even his lips. A nose that had been broken more than once and eyes set deep. He cut into the space around him.

"That's sinful," she said.

If he could have left earlier, if the *Daily News* would have let him stay in one of their kept rooms at a hotel in the city, he would have been gone already, but they made him wait. Lula could sense him vibrating underneath his skin. He could see an exit.

"What about the bird?" Lula asked.

"What about him?"

"Do you expect me to take care of him?"

"Actually, yes. I do," Tom said. "It's not hard."

He walked over to the cage and let the bird out onto his finger. The bird twisted its head around to stare at her. Its neck bent unnaturally, and it made her put a hand up to her throat. Tom stroked it and whispered something that Lula couldn't hear.

The bird loved Tom. It was his bird. Well, not to start with. To start with it belonged to *her*. His wife's bird. During the divorce Lula and Tom had gone on an adventure; that's what he'd called it. They went to the house he had shared with her and broke in. He hadn't planned on it being dramatic as all that, but Margaret had changed the locks like she said she would. A rock the size of his fist got them in. One small broken window above the basement and it became something else.

Lula remembered the way Tom looked at her as if heat burned through his eyes. He helped her down and slid his hands over the length of her, touching every part. When her feet were flat on the ground, he held her there in front of him, against him. And when Lula turned, he had her there—it was the last time it went like that.

They walked right out the front door with the bird still in its cage and that black sheet over it. An African Grey. He had bought it for Margaret in place of an engagement ring. This bird looked as though all the color had been drained from him, everything but the tail which fanned out in a stark red cape. Lula liked the idea of getting Margaret's declaration of love as if it could be transferred over like money in a bank account.

Turned out Margaret couldn't stand the thing either, because she never came after it. Never said a word about it, and she always had a lot to say. This, Lula knew, had gotten under Tom's skin. He was excited the first few days, waiting to hear from Margaret once she came back to town. Said she would fight like a wet cat for that bird. Then the week rolled over to the next. He would ask if she called. Lula would ask why he cared, but she knew. Back in the beginning, when he and Lula had just started, he had told Margaret that the love bites on his neck were from the bird. But the bird never bit him.

***

She read whatever she could find on Ruth and her lover. She hoped she could somehow learn more about them than Tom.

Have an intimate insight into their lives that Tom wouldn't be able to capture and show. Ruth was 32. She was unemployed. She was a mother. Her daughter's name was Lorraine. Her husband's name was Albert. She and her lover, Judd, had killed him. Judd was a corset salesman and losing money. Ruth and Judd held chloroform soaked rags over Albert's mouth and nose. Judd tied a wire around Albert's neck. Judd convinced Ruth to do it so they could be together. Ruth convinced Judd to do it so they could be together. Ruth and Judd had been lovers for two years. Ruth and Judd turned on each other in two hours. All of it Lula memorized. She wanted Tom to quiz her. She wanted him to bring something up, or get something wrong, and if he did, she would gently correct him. "No, that's not what happened; it went like this," she would say. And he would thank her. But Tom didn't talk about it. He just kept checking his backup camera and taking pictures of the bird.

***

She had trouble sleeping when he was gone. Even though they had turned away from each other, his weight in the bed was enough. If not enough, something—a pull she could feel. A reminder in physics. After Tom left, Lula ticked through those facts at night. When she did sleep, she dreamt of Ruth and Judd—but then it wasn't Judd, it was Tom. They stood in a room that had been torn apart, and he stood behind her, tying up her corset before he left. He kissed her in the space between her shoulder blades, grabbing her shoulder as if he wanted to take a part of her with him. Lula would wake up sweating. It reminded her of before. He would do this with Lula when her breathing got caught up and uneven. He would touch her with a kind of determined pressure. He had an agenda. He pawed at her while attempting to disguise it as comfort. He wanted.

But, over time, that pressure she needed had eased. He wouldn't touch her with any of his strength. She braced herself, ready to push back harder against him, but there was nothing. Quickly his hand would be gone altogether, leaving no imprint of where it had been. She used to be able to feel him the next day. Her hips would ache, and she'd stretch until she could feel the soreness. He bruised her neck with his mouth, and she'd open her collar up to the mirror as she examined the marks. Now he didn't leave anything behind.

***

The day that Tom was due back, Lula woke up in the early afternoon, and the bird was squawking. She put the pillow over her head to try and block it out, but it didn't work. She threw the covers off of her and walked to the kitchen to make some coffee. She would not address the bird until she was ready. She would make it wait. When the coffee was ready, she poured it into a little white cup with delicate pink and blue roses on it and a gold painted trim around the rim. Lula had not bought this, it was not her style. She liked plain things—sturdy things. The bird squawked again. It was hungry. On her way out of the kitchen she tripped on the leg of the table, dropping her coffee cup on the ground. The thing seemed to shatter in slow motion, and she didn't move to stop it. The handle flew off like it had torn along a seam.

"Shit," she whispered sharply.

"Shit! Shit!" came back at her from the living room.

The noise the cup made when it fell sounded like it came from inside her skull, and she put her hands over her ears. Lula stepped around the ceramic pieces and walked into the living room, balling up the folds of her robe in her fists. If she kept them free, she'd be liable to swing.

The bird heard her coming, and the cage started to shake. The black sheet with white embroidered vines covered it as it rocked back and forth. A heavy thing, made so the bird wouldn't be able to knock it off on its own.

"Please," Lula said, putting her mouth to the sheet. "Will you please, just, be quiet? I need you to do this for me. Can you? Please?" She breathed out, thinking maybe the hot air from her lungs would do something, like a car in a garage.

"Please! Please!" came from behind the sheet, like a ghost.

The bird's voice came out differently, this time. It sounded more like her, or how she thought she might sound to someone else. Desperate. Something was wrong with it. She wanted to be away from the bird, away from that voice, so she quietly walked to the front door hoping that it wouldn't hear her leave. When she stepped outside, the sun hit her as if interrogating her, and she sank down on the stairs. It was cold and she held her coat tightly to her chest. Her feet were bare but she was testing herself. It was a game; how long could she stand it. She would turn around to keep them moving, and was facing the navy blue door when she heard a car pull up in front of the house. She lifted her head and watched him. Tom paused for a moment, staring at her. He looked as if he'd gotten out at the wrong place. He kept his hand on top of the taxi, then he smiled and reached inside his coat. He pulled out a small bunch of crushed red roses and shook them her direction. He hit the roof and started towards her.

"What are you doing out here?" This was a thing he used to laugh at, but now it was a quick smile. She would have missed it if she had blinked. Thank God.

"I was hot, inside."

"You shouldn't be out here like this."

He opened the door and herded her through it. Inside, the bird started up again. Tom walked over, pulled off the sheet like a magic trick and leaned in.

"Hiya, buddy!" he yelled.

Lula put her hands up to her ears, fearing that her voice would come back out of its beak, but it was silent.

"There's a good man." Tom opened up the wire door and stuck his finger in. The bird marched onto it from its little swing. It flapped its wings and jumped onto Tom's shoulder, then stomped around a bit before settling down. Glad to be home.

"Seems a little stir crazy, must have gotten up early," Tom said, looking from the bird to Lula. His stare was accusatory.

"Excuse me," she said. "I need to wash up."

In the bathroom, she sat on the lid of the toilet with her hands between her knees. She leaned her head against the frosted window, and appreciated its coolness. Lula put her hand to her mouth and started to pick at the dry pieces of skin on her lips. Then she thought about lipstick—if she still had that color he used to like, or if he had ever mentioned liking one in particular.

Lula walked back to the kitchen and stopped in the doorway. She curled her toes to grip the floor. Tom had started another pot with the mess on the floor just inches away from his feet. He had the newspaper tucked into his waistband the way a cop carries a gun. She didn't want to ask about it, but had nothing else to say.

"How did it go, then?"

He turned and smiled at her, the kind of smile she hadn't seen in months. She almost returned it. He grabbed the newspaper and unrolled it. He held it up next to his face as if he were posing with some big game he had hunted.

"Take a look."

Lula couldn't understand at first. It wasn't something she could easily make out. She squinted her eyes causing the pain in her forehead to spread up underneath her hair and across to both temples. She became dizzy. In the picture, Ruth Snyder grabbed both arms of the chair with a grip that she never could have managed before that moment. Her ankles were straining against the leather strap, her feet kicked out to either side. She was wearing black loafers; Lula had a similar pair. Something black covered Ruth's face; it looked like a muzzle made for dogs. The photograph was blurry, and Lula couldn't tell if that was because she could actually see the electricity moving through Ruth's body or if it was the way the picture had been taken. Every sharp line in the photograph couldn't hold its content, the blacks and grays of her were bleeding out. At the bottom of the picture, there was something hard and shiny. A shoe. Tom's shoe. It looked so large and invasive. Right above the photo was a single big, bold word: DEAD!

"You ever seen anything like that?"

"Of course not." Lula rocked a little, placing one cold hand on the wall for balance. She felt as if she had been attacked.

"Here, take a look." Tom brought it close to her face, and she put her hands up.

"Look! Look!" the bird yelled out.

Lula sat down, and Tom grabbed the flowers he had set on the table.

"I'm sorry about these," he said. "They looked more alive when I got them." He started to poke through the petals, seemingly trying to find something in between them. Lula could feel the silk coming off on her fingertips.

"You shouldn't touch them," Lula said, louder than she had meant to.

A rigidness set in his shoulders at the sound of her voice, and she could see his jaw clench.

"What was it like?" she asked.

She saw him relax, and he turned back with a slight smile.

"Fast," he said. He pulled out a chair and sat down hard.

"The guard checked us." His hands were suddenly on her, moving up and down her sides. Lula took in a sharp breath. "Patted us down and let us in the room. I thought he would feel the wire, but you could tell they wanted to get that door closed. Press went to the back of the room, but I shoved up for a good spot where I could see her. Then they brought her in. You could tell she was scared; her lip quivered," he said as he moved his lip with his finger. "And her eyes were wide as planets, but she wasn't crying. They sat her down, strapped her in, then shaved the top of her head."

"Why?" Lula put her hand on top of her own. She imagined a draft.

"They put a wet sponge there." He tapped the top of her head, and she could almost feel her brain shake. "Makes the electrocution go faster, more humane."

"Did she say anything?" she whispered.

"'Forgive them father, for they know not what they do.' Then they flipped it. She grabbed hold of the chair with everything she had, then she went limp. I almost didn't get it in time, but everything lined up perfectly, thank God."

"Thank God." Lula repeated it back to him, slowly but reflexively. She couldn't help herself.

Lula stared at him as he looked over the picture—he couldn't stop smiling. He had caught something special, someone's soul on the outside of their body. He had caught it for himself, and it ignited him. There was nothing in the room now, not even him. He was still there, with Ruth.

"I felt bad for Judd Gray. When they brought him in you could still smell something, like metal. He was weeping and tripping over his feet when they sat him down. She went better than him; that's why they had her go first. They knew she would be better."

"I don't like it," Lula said.

Tom looked at her as if she had hit him.

"She wasn't a saint, you know." He crossed his arms over himself and hardness set back in.

Lula thought Ruth might have been, at the very least, some sort of martyr for herself. Everything had been taken from her and burned up.

"She only had dignity in dying, and that's what I got here."

It was quiet for a moment and then the bird squawked, making Lula's heart jump.

"Can you please get rid of that damn bird?" she said, putting her hands over her ears.

Tom stroked the bird's neck with his finger, then got up from his chair.

"I'm tired," he said with his eyes down. He didn't say anything else right away. The way he had said it sounded almost like a question that she should answer, the way it hung there between them. When he finally did look at her, she stopped breathing, wanting to be as quiet as possible.

"I like the bird," he said, before he turned and walked away. Tom had left the bird on the table. Lula watched it and thought about how stuffy the room felt and how hot it had gotten with the sun coming in. She thought about opening a window while she scratched at her neck. The bird jumped down from the table to the ground so clumsily it surprised her. The bird couldn't fly—its wings were regularly clipped—but she didn't know if it even knew how. It walked over to the puddle of coffee on the linoleum and, with its beak to the floor, stuck its dry, gray tongue out, stabbing at the coffee in a way that made Lula feel sick again, but different—like a smothering. She needed air. Gulps of it.

She had the newspaper in her hand. She didn't know how it got there, really; she must have grabbed it. The paper was thick—special issue heavy. She felt weak and swimmy, but she moved fast. Maybe faster than she had ever moved in her life. She got him on the first swing and it made a terrible noise, and she breathed. She swung again. The sound was a sort of scream that tried to be human but failed and cracked back into something else. It went on like that until it was over. She wished to God it couldn't talk, because even in the silence, with Tom looking at her in the doorway, wet and naked from the shower, she could still hear it ringing in her ears. Lula wondered if that's why they muzzled her.

In 1928, Ruth Synder and her lover Judd Gray murdered Synder's husband, Albert to obtain double indemnity. A life insurance clause that guarantees the beneficiary double if the manner of death is accidental. The plot went sour and the two quickly turned on one another. Both were sent to the electric chair and one clever photojournalist rigged up a camera to his ankle and snapped a picture of Ruth the moment the flick was switched on the electric chair.

"Father, forgive them. They know not what they do."
–Ruth Synder's last words

Chapter Six

Sunvalley Mall, 1985

Let me tell you how I know that Christmas ornaments are more beautiful when they are breaking. When tiny shards of red and green and silver glass spray into the air so small they almost look like dust, but dust is not that pretty. It is almost impossible to explain how cheated I now feel whenever I see perfectly arranged lights or patterned ornaments like red and silver, big and small, all round and intact, when they are so much more stunning broken apart from the whole—burst into chaos.

The same is not true for people. I don't want to tell you how I know that, but the knowledge is interlinked. The two pieces of information hold hands in my memory. Like my father held mine as he dragged me through Macy's to get a gift for my sister Judy, because I knew Santa wasn't real, but she didn't—but she would, soon. The eleven o'clock news would tell her, later.

The skylight, too, like the ornaments, was prettier apart. It rained glass and debris and made everything so impossibly bright. Almost like a miracle. In the air, between the ceiling and the floor, it was as beautiful as what I imagined angels look like, though I didn't think those were real, I would know, soon, that they were, and that they were terrible.

My father covered my eyes when the sound came. It came behind all the light, which I guess it does, but I did not know that then. The sound took my breath away. It was like wind and scream and a vacuum all at once. And breaking, of course. Everything breaking.

What you've heard is true: Angels come from the sky. They travel by twin-engine Beechcraft Barons. They are attracted to sparkling lights, like chandeliers and engagement rings. People rushed them toward water because they flashed up too brightly. Because they are on fire. They were plunged into the fountain in the middle of the mall. The one that was filled with dirty coins and bottle caps. The one my father always gave us change for. Make a wish. It's Christmas.

So I closed my eyes, because everything was so hot then, and I wished for quiet, but what I got was the sound of colored glass, and it sounds just the same as people. Bursting.

Mistaking the mall's skylight for a runway, a twin-engine Beechcraft Baron crashed into the Sunvalley Mall on December 23, 1985. Seven people died—three in the plane and four in the mall. dozens of others were badly burned or injured.

*"Then suddenly at 8:35 p.m., Aguirre heard a
boom above, followed by an instant surge of fire
that ignited her face and hands."*
–Ryan Huff, East Bay Times

Chapter Seven

Love Me Tender

Chicago, IL. 1956

Sam had never listened to Elvis in a room with a bed in it. The realization made her face warm. She only had one radio at her house, and it stood in the living room with mail piled on top. She sat watching the record spin on the tiny pink player, and thought that she had never wanted anything more in her life. She had no idea why the Grimes sisters had it. Their mom had to work just the same as hers. The record sounded different. Like it was just him and her there in the Grimes sisters' all pink bedroom. His voice soaking into all the sheets and blankets and carpet. Barbara and Pat were in the corner by the mirror, putting lipstick on each other at the same time—a trick.

"You're not looking, Sam. See? Not a smudge." Barbara pouted and Pat smiled with her teeth before she saw what her sister was doing and forced her lips closed and similarly pouted. They both looked just like the other one. Sam and her sister looked nothing alike, but Pat and Barbara had the same big mouth that stretched over their faces in the same way. They had the same cheek bones that pushed their eyes way up when they smiled. The same muddy hair cut above their shoulders.

"I can even do it left-handed," said Pat.

"You mess it up," Barbara said.

"No, watch." Pat rubbed her forearm across her mouth, smearing bright red-orange over her cheek.

"Come here, Sam. Let me do you," Barbara said, twisting the lipstick up all the way.

"That's okay," Sam said.

"Come on, this will be a great color on you." She jabbed the tube towards her as if she might stick her with it, leaving a horrible red-orange stain on her chest.

The record ended and continued to scratch through the dust for a few moments until the automatic arm lifted and placed itself neatly to the side in its cradle. Sam turned and reached to flip it over.

"No, we should go downstairs, I'm starving," said Barbara.

At the mention of hunger, Sam remembered Jane. It wasn't like she couldn't feed herself, but she needed to get back before either of her parents did.

"What time is it?" Sam asked.

"I don't know, almost dinner." Barbara shrugged and then her and Pat left the room together, Pat following Barbara as close as a shadow.

Sam was left alone in the room. She felt it already—her fingers shook, or she thought they would be if she looked down, but she never looked. Her heart went faster in her chest and, like all the times before, she couldn't help it—or that's what she told herself. She stole little things that she could fit in her fist—like gum they wouldn't let her chew in school, or pieces of chalk she kept in her underwear drawer but never used. Once she took a girl's ring from the locker room. She watched the girl look for it frantically before feeling so awful she dropped it on the gym floor and pretended to find it. Nothing ever this big. She could still see the record player out of the corner of her eye. She sized it up as best as she could without looking straight at it. If she did that, she would have to fully consider what she was about to do. She threw the record off and then closed the top down, snapping the already rusting locks in place. Then she grabbed the handle, pulling the electrical cord out of the socket, and stuffed the whole thing in her school bag. It fit just fine. Her heart was beating out her ears.

"I have to go home," she said, as she ran towards the front door.

"Oh, okay. We'll see you tomorrow for the movie, right?"

"Yeah, tomorrow."

***

Jane was crying in their room when Sam came in. Jane glared at her with such hurt that Sam had to look at the ground before she signed, "I'm sorry." Jane had to wait for Sam to come home in order to get in the house, and it was cold. She lost the key the week before, and their parents refused to give her another one—she had failed the test of keeping things. Sam heard footsteps coming fast down the hall. The sound of her mother's old work heels hit the wood floor the way a clock ticks down to zero.

"Sam," her mother yelled, already red in the face. She must have come home early from the bank. "I hope you have a good reason for leaving your sister alone for two hours. Look at her lips, they're blue."

"I'm sorry, I just forgot."

"You owe your sister an apology."

When she turned around again, her hand in a fist on her chest, Jane slammed her hand against the bed post, startling both Sam and her mother.

"Jane," her mother said without signing.

"You could at least look at me," Jane said, loudly, with her hands flying around her. "I want another key. I'll be careful."

Their mother put her finger up to her lips and quietly shushed, she couldn't help making the noise. Jane shot up from the bed and stomped out of the room, trying to find the unobstructed path in-between Sam and their mother. Their mother timidly reached out, but Jane was too far gone down the hallway. She brought her hand back to her mouth, putting a nail between her teeth. Without looking at her other daughter, their mother slammed the bedroom door and clicked away.

Sam was on the verge of crying. One small push in her throat could get the whole thing started, but when she touched the strap of her bag, she remembered what she had and she almost laughed. She took it off her shoulder and pressed her back against the door. She peered inside and there it was, waiting for her. She pulled it out and slid down on her butt to hold it in her lap. She ran her fingers on the hard leather case, and then came to the scotch tape where either Barbara or Pat had written in big, black capital letters "GRIMES." She started to dig a fingernail underneath the tape when she heard another set of footsteps coming up the stairs. They were heavy. She pushed the record player under her bed and then quick sat on top of the covers, facing the wall. Her father pushed the door open with his fingers.

"Sam," he said.

"Yes, daddy?"

"Where were you today?"

"I forgot, that's all. I went over to the Grimes' and I just forgot. As soon as I remembered I came right home."

"What if something happened?"

"I know, daddy, I honestly just forgot. Can't I make a mistake sometimes?"

"It wouldn't be smart for you to pick up an attitude at this moment, Sam."

"Yes, daddy."

"Come here."

She slid off the bed and walked over to him. He put his meaty hand on her shoulder and sighed.

"I know it's hard, with . . . I know you want to do whatever you like, but none of us get that luxury, no matter what circumstances . . ." He was struggling and she wanted to say something to end the whole thing, but her tongue was stuck in her mouth.

"No radio after dinner, tonight. It's homework and bed."

She nodded again, wondering how she'd get the record upstairs without out bending itself under her shirt.

***

Sam waited in her quiet house for what felt like hours before she got out of bed and reached underneath for the record player. She found the cord and pulled at it slowly, trying not to let the metal corners scratch against the floor. She grabbed the record out from under her sheets and wiped the dust off with her palm. She plugged it in and turned the dial. A pop came out of the speakers louder than she had expected. A strong hum followed and she realized she needed to find a way to muffle the sound. She pulled her quilt off the bed and then went to the far back corner of the room, stretching the record player as far as it could go, and put the quilt over herself and the player like a tent. She needed to make sure she wasn't moving too much, so Jane wouldn't feel her vibrations and wake up. She wouldn't tell, but she'd want to sit with her, too, and pretend to listen. She'd bob her big head and rock her body on the ground, but she wouldn't know what she was doing, not really. Jane liked the way it felt when she put her hand against the speaker in the living room, and she often tried to get Sam to do the same, forgetting it made the music harder to hear.

Sam carefully placed the record down on the spindle, then lifted up the arm and dropped it at the very edge. His voice came first, no instruments. Just him and her in there for the length of six words. By the time it got to "I Love You Because," Sam was on her back with her knees holding the blanket up, moving her hips and squeezing her thighs together. Picturing the way his face looked on the cover, the way his eyes were closed and his mouth was open. His hair was wet and his jacket bunched up around his guitar. His fingers curled around the neck of it, except the pinky which stood straight out. Sam tried to keep still until the end, but she couldn't. Then, after, she stayed there until Blue Moon came on, her skin hot, her face and hands damp as she continued to breathe in her own air, making herself warmer. The last song sounded like he was singing into a tin can, and the strangeness roused her to sit up and hug her knees as it finished. It was getting uncomfortable under the blanket. She stuck a hand out and felt the cool, thin air of their bedroom.

***

Sam's parents wanted her to take Jane to the movie with the Grimes sisters. Sam didn't want to go at all. The Grimes sisters had to know by now. She waited all morning for the phone to ring. She'd know it was them before her mother picked up—the sound of the ring would be off, somehow. Her mother would answer with a smile and then it would leave when she asked, "what's missing?" But they didn't call. At the very least, if Sam had to go and be interrogated at the movies, she could keep Jane out of it.

"She can't even hear it," Sam whispered. She knew this was too awful to say loudly.

Her father stared at her from the kitchen table, taking deep, exaggerated breaths while he waited to speak.

"She likes them, anyway, Sam," her mother said as she drank her coffee.

"Then she'll get loud, she always gets too loud during. I can't explain what's happening in the dark, and she just gets mad and wants to leave. Daddy, I've been waiting to see this movie all my life, can't I just go without her? I'll take her to see something else, soon, I promise."

"After yesterday, you're lucky you're still going. I thought you were sorry."

"I am sorry, daddy," Sam whined.

He slammed his fist on the table, "You're a brat is what you are, if Jane didn't want to see this so badly you'd be in your room for the rest of the weekend."

Sam walked into the hallway and up the stairs, crying and stepping as loud as she could. She heard her father shut the sliding kitchen door hard enough that it bounced back and he had to do it twice. Sam got into her room and slammed the door behind her. Jane looked up excited and happy until she saw her sister's face. Sam flopped down on her bed and stared up at the ceiling, and Jane came over her.

"I'll be good," she signed. "I promise."

Sam stared at her for a moment before signing, "Just don't talk, okay? Really try not to."

Jane nodded her head, smiling.

"Okay, then, let's go," Sam said.

Jane reached for Sam's hand.

"Just in the house, and when we're crossing the street, okay?"

Jane nodded again. Sam took her hand, though she wanted to pull away, but this was the deal. Jane held tightly, her nails digging into the thin skin between Sam's knuckles. When they were at the front door, their father peeked out from the kitchen and smiled at them—well, no, at Jane, alone.

"Come here," he said, gesturing with a single finger when he had used a whole fist just before.

Jane dragged Sam with her as she jumped up and kissed him on the check. He rubbed her head and signed, "Have fun. Tell me what it was like when you get home—but don't spoil the ending for me, okay, kid?"

Jane laughed and yelled, "goodbye," too loud as she started out the door, and Sam cringed.

"Get her home safe, Sam."

"Sure, Dad."

"Hey, wait," he said. "Take this for some popcorn and whatever else you want. Don't get too full on that stuff, though. Mom's making spaghetti tonight. Come home right after." He handed her five dollars. She wondered if she'd be able to keep the rest of it. If he'd even notice.

***

Elvis stood so perfectly tall above everything else on the poster. He didn't look like a cowboy, even though it was supposed to be a western. He was playing his guitar and singing out of the side of his mouth, while another one of him kissed a girl on the cheek with his eyes open. She had red, red lipstick on with dark eyebrows—darker than her hair.

Jane was staring, too. She reached up her hand and touched it, tracing Elvis's name with her finger. Sam saw her lips start to form the name, her tongue trying to work it out in her mouth, her chest rising up to push the wind out to make the noise.

"Come on," Sam said, tugging on her sister's wrist. "It's time to go in."

Sam's heart beat quick in her chest as they bought popcorn and soda. She thought about Barbara and Pat waiting to confront her in perfect unison, just like the way they did lipstick. Sam and Jane were ushered in by a painfully blond boy in braces. Barbara and Pat were already in their seats, waiting for them in the dark. Barbara stuck up her hand and waved.

"Here!" Barbara yelled.

People in the audience shushed her.

"Oh, the movie hasn't even started yet," Barbara said.

Pat shoved Barbara in her seat and shushed her louder than she had spoken. Sam and Jane settled in behind them, and the Grimes sisters turned in their seats. Sam held her breath.

"Hi, Jane," Pat whispered, waving.

"Hi!"

More shushing from other seats. Sam slapped Jane's knee and fiercely signed, "be quiet." And then drew her finger across her throat. They would have said something by now, Sam thought. Neither one of them was any good at containing themselves. Just then, the movie started with music loud enough to shake their seats, and Sam almost spit out her soda. In pretty letters, Sam saw the names of the actors she didn't know, one underneath the other on top of the screen. Below them popped up, "And Introducing Elvis Presley."

It took too long for him to come on. Jane asked for some dots and Sam was fishing one out with her finger when Jane gasped.

She almost missed him, but then there, small at first, in the distance, then up real close. When he first sang, she got a feeling in her middle, just below her heart where her ribs came together. Girls in the audience screamed, throwing their dark heads back and clapping their hands over their mouths. Sam didn't want to scream. It was too public. At one point, she looked at Pat in front of her, and she could see that she was saying something. Sam bent forward to hear her, but she wasn't speaking, she just moving her lips, and that's when Sam realized she was miming the words to the movie. They had seen it before.

Barbara leaned back without taking her eyes off the screen. "Close your eyes, this is the worst part."

Instead of keeping her eyes up on the movie, she watched them fall all apart when they killed him, grasping onto each other's hands and sobbing. Then, at his own funeral, he came back on screen, all see-through like a ghost, singing the same song but dressed up in a suit. He smiled when he finished. His lips were so big. All the girls smiled back.

The four of them walked out of the theater together, blinking at the bright lobby lights.

"We should go, we're going to miss the bus," Sam said.

"Oh, we don't have to go yet," Barbara said. "Mom said we could stay for two showings."

"You mean you're seeing it twice?"

"Yup, uh huh," Pat said.

"Well, do you think you should?" *That's not fair*, she meant.

"What do you mean?" Barbara laughed. "We've seen it ten times already."

Empty and defeated, all Sam could say was, "see you later."

"See ya!" Pat yelled.

Jane reached out her hand but Sam left it alone. *That's not fair.*

***

That night, Sam left the record player under her bed and imagined him next to her, propped up on his elbow, holding her hand, and singing to her. She could never have thought up all the ways he moved and talked like that. The whole experience made her realize that she hadn't really known him at all, though she thought she knew him well. The way he had grabbed the woman, fiercely, every part of him filled with desperation and passion. Romance was the only word that would work for what was underneath his skin. How he got so jealous and mean when it all became too much for him.

With the blanket pulled up over her head, Sam put her hand on her stomach and closed her eyes. She pretended it was his hand and she moved it side to side, lighting trailing a finger or two so she could trick herself into being tickled. She moved it up her ribs to her too small breasts and pretended that they were bigger, as full as that woman's, and she squeezed them with his hand.

"Sam," Jane said.

Sam's breath caught in her mouth and she swallowed it. She sat up and put her finger to her lips. Jane covered her mouth for a moment and laughed.

"Can you tell me if this sounds right?" Jane signed.

Sam nodded, signing, "Whisper."

"El-vish," Jane said.

Sam put her hand in a fist for "s," then signed "like snake."

"Oh, like Sam." Jane pointed to her and smiled.

Sam nodded. "Like me."

***

Mr. Grimes pounded at their door at midnight. Both Sam and Jane followed their parents down the hallway but stayed crouched on the stairs. When Sam saw him, she almost started to cry. He was there for the record player, she knew it.

"What is it, Bob?" Sam's father said as the girls waited behind their mother on the stairs.

"The girls aren't here, are they Rick?"

Rick shot a look over his shoulder on reflex, before realizing.

"No, they're not here. What happened?"

"They never came home after the movies. I know they went with your girls." Mr. Grimes made his way into the house, and their own father stepped away as if he were scared of him. The girls squeezed closer together against the railing, and Sam could feel the cold from outside come between the spindles.

"Sam and Jane were home at nine."

"They stayed for the second showing," Sam said from the stairwell, and it seemed to echo in the front hall.

"What?" Mr. Grimes asked.

Sam was snitching, but she thought it served them right.

"They told us it was okay if they stayed."

"You mean you girls didn't stay with them?"

Sam shook her head. "We weren't allowed, Mr. Grimes."

"We only let them stay later because we thought the two of you were. We wouldn't have let them stay so late by themselves, you know?" Mr. Grimes looked towards their father who blinked the blank stare off of his face and replaced it with a stern nod.

"Ah, Christ." Mr. Grimes wiped his big hand down his face, as if he were trying to straighten out his features, but no matter what he did he still looked terrified.

***

Two days later, Sam's parents were listening to the radio while she read on the floor when they heard, again, about the Grimes sisters. It came through as a special bulletin, the man's voice suddenly very serious and harsh sounding in their small living room.

"They were last seen on December 28th, standing in line at the Brighton Theater at S. Archer and Sacramento, after seeing *Love Me Tender* with two friends. Both girls stayed for a second showing and were expected home late, but never showed up at their bus stop. Barbara Grimes is 15, and Patricia Grimes is 13. They live in McKinley Park with their mother and father who are both terribly worried. The girls are big fans of Elvis Presley and they've talked about running away to Nashville with their friends. If any of you out there know these girls or where they might be, please help get them home by telling the police."

She could see her parents collectively sigh, and she wondered if it was because the radio didn't mention that it was their own children were with them. That their children were the last to see them. It was Sunday and school would be starting soon. There was a kind of dread sitting in the pit of Sam's stomach. She would have to walk into school as if she were diseased, like she had touched something dirty and they all knew. She tried to prepare herself and practice how she might answer their questions. *Yes, we were with them. No, they didn't seem strange. No, they didn't talk about running away to Nashville, but I can't really remember what they did say.* She didn't, either. She tried, and when she thought back to it, she couldn't pick out anything that might make for a coded message. A secret goodbye of some kind. She didn't have anything to do with it. That's all she wanted to say. She tried to picture them in Nashville, but she didn't know what Nashville looked like. All she could see was them standing in the cold on the corner of their street, dressed in summer clothes.

She rolled over on the ground and put her hand on her stomach, wondering if she started faking it now if she could maybe stay home, but talking to her parents had become strange and suspect, as if even they thought she knew something she wasn't saying. They'd try and sneak in questions when she wasn't expecting them. In the morning, when she was tired and brushing her teeth, her mother came to the bathroom door.

"Sam, sweetheart, did they say anything to you?"

With the toothbrush still in her mouth she shook her head.

"Some people are saying that they were talking with a young man who, well, they said he kind of looked like Elvis, you know, black hair. Did you see anyone like that there?"

"No, mom. I didn't see anyone, I swear."

Her mother stared at her for a moment before she smiled.

"You're a good girl, Sam."

The staring was unnerving. They looked at both her and Jane for longer. Her mother reached out to stroke Jane's hair from behind, and Jane would jump because she didn't see her coming. Neither parent wanted them to leave the house, and Sam was no longer trusted to be the short-term guardian. On New Years, the four of them stayed home. Her mother fell asleep on the couch still dressed up with her stocking covered legs dangling, her muscles jerking every few minutes. Nobody was sleeping well. The worst part came at the end of the night, when Sam and Jane both went to bed. They stood outside their daughters' room, looking into the dark from the doorway with the dim orange hallway light behind them. Their dark heads turned from one bed to the other while Sam watched through the thin slit of her eyes. She kept still, not wanting to give them a reason to come in. She let them hover there like ghosts until they both reluctantly and slowly creeped away.

The record player sat underneath her bed, unplayed. She didn't touch it. She thought, soon, her parents would find it. She'd come home one day and see it sitting out on the kitchen table with her mother and father glaring at her. The "GRIMES" label still stuck on there. The word traced and retraced over again in black. She didn't let her toes disappear underneath where it waited. When she would wake up at night with an arm hanging over the bed, she'd snap it back to her chest. *I'll return it*, she said to herself. *When they come home, I'll give it back.* Later, when she would feel so awful about the record player that she couldn't sleep, she would think back to this moment and remind herself that she would've made it better if she had been given a chance.

***

If you are good Presley fans, you'll go home and ease your mother's worries.

Sam's mouth hung open and Jane stared at her.

"What's the matter?" Jane signed.

His voice had rolled over every word as if he were warming up his throat. She sat up from the floor onto her knees.

"Well, isn't that something," her dad said.

"What's that?" her mom asked.

"Elvis Presley just came on the radio and talked about the Grimes girls."

"Really?"

"Just now, asked them to go home to their mother."

"That's kind of him. Wonder how he knows."

"Me, too. Though, I'm sure the Nashville police were informed—in case." He shut quickly closed his mouth and glanced at Sam.

"What's the matter, sweetheart?" he asked her.

Sam didn't say anything for a moment. She put her hand over her mouth as an unwanted smile started to appear. She had the strangest feeling. She wanted to giggle. She breathed through her nose, counting to six, as her father cocked his head a little and stared, his face getting more and more worried looking. Watching him made it worse and her other hand clapped over her mouth. Sam got up and ran to the small downstairs bathroom. The door shut harder than she had meant it to and it rattled the little mirror above the sink.

She caught her reflection behind the water stains and got closer to it. Did Elvis know about her then? He could have been talking about her—to her. She strained her eyes to find the ways her and the Grimes sisters looked the same. Her hands still up near her face, she tucked her hair behind her ears so she could see more. Her color was the almost the same dark brown as theirs. Sam smiled with her mouth open. Pat had her braces off three months before, and she liked to show off her teeth. Yes, she thought—he could have been talking about her. She felt like running away.

***

They were found without clothes on. "These flesh colored things," is how the man said it to the paper. The snow melted and their bodies were uncovered in a ditch on the side of the road next to a guardrail. They were frozen. Sam heard her mom talking about it over the phone. The man first thought they were mannequins. Their bodies were intertwined, with Pat covering Barbara who was curled up to hold her knees. When Jane asked their father how they died, he said, "exposure," loudly, and

Jane got angry, shaking her head side to side. He couldn't think of the word in sign language. He looked at Sam for help.

"What does "exposure" mean?" she asked.

Their father rolled his eyes in frustration.

"It means, you know, the outside elements killed them. Like how you can't live outside?"

"Because it's cold?"

He clapped his hands together and pointed at her. "Yes, that's exactly it."

Sam turned to Jane and put her two fists up in "s"s and then shook them fast.

"Cold?" Jane asked.

Sam nodded, thinking it would never be so cold in Nashville.

***

That night, their parents didn't stay as long in the doorway. It was as if they had all been holding their breath for a very long time and then finally let it go. They went to their own room and shut the door. None of the lights were left on. Sam laid there in the dark trying not to hear that subtle rushing noise she heard when it was very quiet. She hadn't moved in her bed, meaning the sheets around her were ice. She thought about stinging, wet snow melting in a cast of her body. When her heart started to beat faster, she opened her eyes and got up. Jane sat up in her bed, too.

"Sam," she said.

Sam didn't answer, she closed the door and started pulling her blankets off the bed. She scrambled underneath for the record player. Her hands were shaking worse than when she had taken it from them, but she forced herself to look their name scribbled on tape that she could somehow see in the dark.

"Sam," Jane said again, this time getting up.

Sam put her finger over her lips and hissed at her through her teeth, almost stomping at her.

"Let me go under there," Jane said.

"Under where?" Sam asked.

"The blankets, I want to listen, too."

The two of them stood there, staring at one another.

"Okay," Sam said.

She put the record player between both of their feet and put the blanket over both of their heads. She opened it up and placed the record on it. She grabbed Jane's hand and placed it on the needle. Jane put it down in the middle, and put her hand against the small speaker. Sam couldn't hear what song started playing, but that was okay. She felt warmer with her sister close.

Just after Christmas in 1956, sisters Barbara, 15, and Patricia, 12 went to see an Elvis movie in Chicago, IL, with friends and were never seen alive again. Two weeks later, their bodies were found along the side of the road, naked, nearly mistaken for roadkill. The time in between their disappearance and discovery of their bodies saw a national outcry for answers, including a statement from Elvis Presley, imploring the girls to return home.

Their case remains unsolved.

*"If you are good Presley fans, you'll go home and
ease your mother's worries."*
–Elvis Presley

Chapter Eight

The Book of Ruth

Kirtland, OH. 1989

The first thing Dolly noticed about her daughter was not the hole in her tooth, but her hair. It went all the way to the tops of her thighs. She could have tucked it into her back pockets. Clementine, or Tiny, as they called her until just before she left them, stood on the front porch with her stringy, long brown hair and her khaki skirt that went down to her shoes and her white shirt that buttoned all the way up, making Dolly pull at the skin of her own neck. She hadn't seen her daughter in two years. It was not without trying. The fluorescent porch light turned her daughter's pale skin a shade of blue.

"Hello, mother."

Tiny's voice sounded deeper. Dolly wondered if female voices did that between ages 18 and 20. Dolly wondered if her daughter started smoking. She stepped forward and put her daughter's face in her hands, coming very close because she couldn't help herself. Tiny went stiff but didn't pull away, and Dolly could feel her daughter's jaw clench against her palms. She found more differences. Slight changes around her daughter's eyes and mouth—her lips seemed thinner. She had more spots now, light and dark, dotting her cheeks and nose and forehead. A very dark one had developed in the middle of her chin. Dolly brought her daughter closer and buried her face into Tiny's neck. She breathed her in until she thought she would faint. She smelled different, almost antiseptic, but underneath there was something familiar. Maybe Tiny was sweating or producing oils on her skin in order to make it easier to slip from her mother's boney hands, but Dolly knew that smell and her grip was strong.

Finally, Tiny put her hands up to her mother's arms—not moving them away, but a warning.

"Is it okay if I stay here? I don't know for how long. Is that okay?"

Dolly laughed and at that moment the wind came, blowing some of Tiny's hair into her mouth. She pulled it out. That was when Dolly saw the small black hole in her daughter's canine, eroding the edge and slowly splitting the tooth apart.

"Tiny, baby, of course it is. This is your home. We've been waiting for you to come home."

"It's Ruth, actually." Tiny let her arms fall as her mother kept holding her. Tiny attempted to back up.

"Oh, still?"

"Still, yes."

Before she left them, before the hole, she asked her parents to call her Ruth.

"I'm not a miner's daughter, I'm God's daughter," she had said at dinner. Dolly knew her daughter thought this was clever.

Her father laughed, but Dolly also knew then that the fracture between them had worsened. Grown deeper while she wasn't looking.

"I think I'll stick with Clementine, Tiny," her father said. Dolly didn't say anything, trying to commit herself to not using a name at all.

"I lie at the feet of *Him*, like Ruth."

"That's enough of that talk," her father said. Dolly continued her silence and two weeks later, Ruth was gone.

"That's fine," Dolly said, smiling. She brought her daughter into the house and locked the door behind her, as if that had stopped her before. Tiny stood in the middle of the living room, surveying the things around her. Dolly wondered what had changed, if anything, since she left.

"Do you want anything to eat? Or do you want to put your things away?" It was a stupid question, Tiny didn't have anything with her, and she lifted her empty hands in demonstration.

"That's alright, everything is in your room."

"My room?"

"Of course. All your clothes, your records, books, whatever. It's all still there."

"Oh," Tiny said.

***

Tiny was their only child, and Dolly thought this was why Tiny didn't sleep in her own room until high school. When she was young, still just a toddler, it was easy to let her stay in their bed. Don pretended and put up a show of annoyance, but when he realized no one was watching, that it was just the three of them in that little house, he let her in-between them and everybody slept better. When she got older, she tried harder at sleeping alone. She would start off in her own bed, but then, sometime during the night, she would end up outside their open door, waiting in the dark to be invited.

Then, it seemed like it happened in one night, she became doggedly possessive of her space. The room that had been decorated the same since she was three; a pink flowered quilt, plain white walls, baskets of toys and things on shelves—transformed into something else, something older. Tiny grew in there, alone. And despite that she no longer came to their door at night, Dolly kept it open, always waiting. Dolly started having trouble sleeping.

***

"How about I make you a sandwich? We have some cold cuts in the fridge, and some mayo."

"Did you paint in here?" Tiny asked.

"Of course not," Dolly lied.

"I remember it different."

"I'm going to make us some sandwiches. I have some iced tea, too. Would you like some?" Dolly asked but was really saying: *please please stay, I'll keep it all the same for you, please.*

"Does it have caffeine?"

"No, I don't think so," Dolly said, but she didn't really know. After Tiny left, she kept up the things she wanted for a few months. No caffeine or booze in the house, the Bible stayed out on the coffee table. She kept working on the cross stitch of a passage from the book of Ruth: *Do not urge me to leave you or to return from following you. For where you go I will go, and where you lodge I will lodge. Your people shall be my people, and your God my God.* She meant it as a kind of plea to her daughter, but it was not taken. After some time, her husband brought home some beer and they had it at dinner. Then the Bible was put away.

"I'll just have some water."

"Sure."

She pulled out an old cup from the cabinet. It had a kissing Donald and Daisy on it with hearts floating up that were almost scratched away. When she finished making the sandwiches she set the cup with the image facing towards her daughter, hoping to incite a comment. Tiny didn't notice. It had been her favorite cup, even in high school. The only thing she'd wash herself if it was dirty. Dolly watched her throat move as she drink, her cheeks slightly puffing in and out with each gulp. Tiny finished it all at once.

"Do you want some more?"

"Yes, please." She pushed the glass toward her mother and then left her hand out. The palm was calloused and looked much harder than it had, but then again, Dolly couldn't really remember her hands before, all she could think of was the way they were when Tiny was a baby. Of course, they had grown and hardened since then. She picked up the cup and went over to the sink. Behind her, her daughter moved. She couldn't see what she was doing, but Tiny was shifting or stirring, quietly, as if she was trying not to be heard. Dolly turned around and saw her daughter scraping the skin away from her thumb nail. She stretched it until it bled and then put her whole thumb in her mouth and sucked it like an infant—something she had never done. Tiny caught her mother staring and dropped it then wiped it against her cheek.

"Where is he?"

Dolly brought over the glass and set it in front of her daughter as she sat down across from her, again. Tiny's eyes were trained on her, peering through thin slits with her hands in her lap.

"He's still at work, should be home in about an hour." Dolly rubbed her palm against the table as she said, "Oh, he'll be so happy to see you." She wished she could have held her daughter's hand to keep her thumb out of her mouth, but she kept them to herself.

***

When they had gone to the Lundgren farm a few weeks after Tiny left, she was kept away, or maybe she kept herself away. They had waited because Don had said she'd come back when she realized how good she had it at home. When everything wasn't being done for her. Dolly didn't think so, and finally Don relented. Dolly went to the door alone. It was a big white farmhouse with a long, dirty porch, and she stepped around the pieces of a broken chair spread out on the floorboards. She pressed her finger down on the doorbell, but nothing happened so she knocked. She heard hard footsteps coming and she looked at Don sitting in the car in the driveway. He was watching her.

"Who's there?" The voice was low and strong on the other side of the door. If it had been any louder it might have caused a slight vibration in Dolly's chest.

"Hello?"

"Who's there?"

"This is Dolly Miller. I'm Clementine's mother."

Then the door opened and he stepped out onto the porch. Jeff Lundgren was fat and Dolly hadn't expected that. His hair was long and slicked back, showing off how it was receding away from his forehead. His skin was pockmarked and shiny, and he was tall, but very fat. He stepped forward, coming too close. She looked, again, to Don in the car and he finally got out. The man didn't even blink when the car door shut. Instead he put his hand forward, the tips of his fingers almost grazing her stomach. She sucked in deeply.

"My name's Jeff." He kept still.

She took her hand out of her glove and backed up in order to put it in his.

"Dolly Miller. Like I said, I'm Clementine's mom."

"Clementine?"

"We're here for our daughter," Don said, coming up behind Dolly.

Jeff let go of Dolly's hand and extended his to Don. Don eyed it before shaking it hard.

"That's a good grip, Mister . . ."

"Miller. You know, the same as Clementine."

"I'm sorry, as I was just about to tell your wife, I don't have anybody here by that name."

"You do, we know you do. She told us about you before she left. About this." Her voice was too high. In the house behind him she imagined many women dressed all the same. Their hair back in a single braid. And when she thought of Tiny in there, she thought of her when she was seven and had learned how to braid, braiding everything she found.

"I'm sorry, ma'am, I'm being honest."

"Ruth, what about a Ruth?" Don asked with his eyes closed.

"Ah." Jeff smiled and winked—a trick, then. "Ruth. Ruth is staying with us, me and my wife and children, and others like her who want to get closer to God."

"Sure," Don said.

"Can we see her? Can you send her out?"

"I can't make her do anything she doesn't want to."

"That's some horseshit if I ever heard. I know people like you; con artists, cheats. You can convince weaker people to do anything you want."

"Don," Dolly said.

"Get my daughter you piece of shit or I'll come in there myself." Don brustled up closer and taller, and Dolly saw he had the same gut Jeff had. She had no clue when he had gotten so big.

"Now, sir, Ruth is a strong adult. Not so weak as you think. She can leave whenever she wants. We love her and respect her here, which is something she says she was missing in her life. But, if you continue to trespass or attempt to gain entry to my home, I'm afraid I'll have to call the police."

"The police? I should be calling them on you for kidnapping!"

"Ruth came here to us in search of help and home. And, I'm sure I don't have to remind you, but she ain't no kid."

Don went forward to hit him, but Dolly grabbed onto his arm and he almost lifted her off the ground.

"Don! Stop, this isn't going to help anything."

Jeff flinched then and Don put his arm down. He stormed back to the car and Jeff watched before he turned back to Dolly, suddenly smiling, as if he had been the whole time.

"I'll let Ruth know that you all came by." He went back in house and slammed the door.

Dolly stood alone on the porch for a moment. It was quiet even though she strained to hear behind the walls. She listened for her daughter's voice but heard nothing.

***

Dolly stared at her daughter across the table, willing her to smile in the little way she used to when she was trying to keep her happiness contained. But she only rolled her eyes.

"Right," Tiny said. "I'm sure he'll be."

"He will be. He's missed you so much. We both have."

Tiny looked at the ground. This was making her uncomfortable.

"Are you okay? Are you tired?"

"I'm fine."

The phone rang, sounding unbearably loud. Tiny's eyes grew wide.

"I'm not here, okay? Please don't tell anyone I'm here."

"Okay, baby. I'm sure it's just a telemarketer."

Dolly thought her daughter was going to cry. Tiny started biting around the inside of her mouth. Dolly wanted to stay with her and smooth her very long hair. The phone rang at least ten times before she finally tore herself from the kitchen table and picked it up.

"Hello?"

There was a click, and then silence, and then the dial tone came. She hung up and walked back to the table.

"Who did you think it would be?" Dolly asked her daughter.

"Nobody." Tiny began picking up the crumbs around her sandwich with her index finger.

"You can tell me."

"I don't live here. I don't know who calls."

***

After the visit to the farm, Dolly and Don went to the police station. The officer they talked to, Dolly couldn't remember his name after he told it to her, said they'd had troubles with Jeff Lundgren before. Gunshots going off at the house, theft, trespassing. They'd talked to him several times, and he always backed down.

"Backed down from what?" Don asked.

"His threats, or whatever he calls them. His prophesizing."

"His what?"

"He says he can talk to God directly, and he gives instructions to all his followers as if he himself were Jesus Christ. Never heard of Jesus needing all that money, or all that company.

Dolly thought she might get sick.

"The women especially get sucked in by him. They're all in love with him, worship him, sleep with him, do whatever he wants. He hangs up a sheet in the woods and hides behind it while they dance naked out there in the dark," this he whispered, leaning closer to Don. "One of them, not his wife, came up and slapped one of my deputies in the face last time we went over there. They guard him like dogs. He's lucky we didn't take her in. Figured she's not exactly in her right mind, if you get me. None of them are, over there."

"What about our daughter?" Don asked through his teeth.

"Ah, my mouth, no one needs to hear that. Really, it's a shame, I'm sorry about that, but there's nothing we can do. She's over 18, sir. Just pray she'll wake up and see that man for what he is."

Dolly wanted to explain to this man how impossible that was. Tiny was joyful, but so naïve. She took things on their face and held them there always. She had never asked about made up things because she never questioned them. Once, she found her Christmas presents in the back of Dolly's closet. She was staring right at the pink plastic sled she had asked for after seeing it at the mall, and all she said was, "oh!" Quickly, Dolly said "sometimes he has to drop off presents ahead of time, if he's in the neighborhood." Her daughter kept smiling, and responded with, "I know that, mom." Though, of course, she didn't know.

***

Tiny ate the sandwich slowly. She was not starving and this almost disappointed Dolly. She took small bites and chewed them for too long before taking another. Dolly could hear her daughter swallow. The hole in her daughter's tooth showed itself only once or twice while she ate and Dolly thought maybe this was why it was taking so long. Tiny had to be careful because her teeth were rotting.

The phone rang again, but the air in the room had changed and as if watching cracking glass Dolly was braced for the break in silence, this time. She grabbed the phone off the hook in the middle of the second ring, but instead of saying "hello," she just watched her daughter's face. The person on the other end was quiet. Dolly heard them part their lips and push them back together and swallow. Then they hung up.

"Mom?" Tiny asked, softly.

"Yes, baby?"

"He's so angry."

"Did he do something to you?"

"He wouldn't," Tiny said, but she said it to herself. She looked at the red skin she'd scratched away at her thumb and Dolly could tell her daughter wasn't breathing.

"Am I different now?" Tiny asked.

"Of course not," Dolly said, lying again.

"He loves us all, even those children—it just had to be."

The front door swung open and shut inside of a second and both women held their breath.

Don said, "Someone just standing in the middle of the road out there, high as a goddam kite, wouldn't move when I got close and I almost had to drive up on the grass getting around them."

He came into the kitchen and Dolly couldn't see his face, but she could hear the way his body went when he saw his daughter at the table.

"Tiny," he said.

"Ruth," Dolly said. "Please."

Don swallowed and then squared his shoulders.

"Sure. Ruth."

"Hi, dad."

"Hi."

"Come sit down, Don."

"Are you home, now?" Don asked.

"For now," Tiny said.

He came to the table, to the chair next to his daughter, and he pulled it out so he was sitting in the middle of the kitchen, far away from both of them.

"When you're done here, are you going back there?"

"Don, we don't need to figure this out yet," Dolly said.

"No. I can't." When Tiny said it, something caught in her throat and there was a break in her voice. Don ran his hand down his face and then put his hands on his knees as he got up. He was getting older and Dolly hadn't noticed. She wondered if it was a shock to Tiny, but her daughter wasn't watching.

"Well, then, we won't talk about it in this house. When you're here, you won't talk about it. Understand me?"

Tiny stared at him, almost glaring, before she nodded.

"Good. I'm sure your mother told you, everything's as it was in your room."

"Yes," Tiny said. "Thank you. I'm tired, do you mind if I go to bed, mother?"

"Do whatever you like," Don said.

"Are you sure you don't want to talk more?" Dolly asked.

"She said she's tired."

"Don, Jesus Christ." Dolly whipped around and narrowed her eyes at him.

Don opened his mouth and then shut it.

"Now, do you want to tell me something, Ruth?" Dolly asked.

Tiny stood and shook her head.

"I'm tired, is it alright if I just go to bed?"

"Sure. Maybe tomorrow we can call the dentist, too, yeah?" Don asked

There was a moment where it seemed as if her daughter wanted to jump out of her own skin, and Dolly desperately wanted to keep her all together.

"That's fine, baby. Okay," Dolly said.

Tiny left and Dolly heard her room door shut softly. She had never shut it like that, before. She was reckless with the way she would close it, always too excited, and she moved part of the frame out of place over time. That part was still off. Alone in the kitchen, Dolly went over to the sink to wash her daughter's dishes for the first time in two years. She scrubbed them with her hands instead of the sponge, touching all the parts her daughter touched. Outside the kitchen window, she saw someone walking slowly up the sidewalk, past their house. She did not know them. She turned her back to the window and leaned against the sink. She was waiting for the phone to ring—she felt it coming through the hairs on her arms. She rushed to it, snatching it off the hook and then letting it drop on the floor. It twisted around like a snake on the tile and when she heard the dial tone beeping, she shut off the lights and walked down the hallway into her own bedroom. Don was awake in the dark, she could tell, but she didn't speak to him. She took off her clothes and crawled into bed, keeping a distance of inches of cold sheets between them. After a while of listening for movement from her daughter's room on the other side of the wall, and hearing nothing but the silence that had been there before, her body relaxed and she drifted off to sleep.

It was still dark when she woke up, and she had the sense that she had just been having a very vivid dream, but she couldn't remember it. She was about to turn over and put her arm around her husband when she saw a shadow on the wall next to her bed. It shifted slightly, but didn't get bigger or smaller, just swayed. She watched it for a little while until she couldn't bare it anymore and shut her eyes. She shut them tightly, hoping her daughter couldn't see her face from where she stood in the doorway. Dolly breathed slow and shallow, trying to listen for her daughter's breath, but she couldn't hear it. Maybe, her daughter wasn't there at all, but Dolly didn't want to know. She kept her eyes closed.

In 1989 there was a small Ohio cult, branched off from the Reorganized Church of Jesus Christ of Latter-Day Saints, led by Jeffrey Lundgren. Lundgren claimed that God demanded a sacrifice and murdered one entire family, the Avery Family: two adults and three children. Other cult members were involved with varying levels of guilt and intent. Eight months after the murders, a dissatisfied member turned on Lundgren and Lundgren was arrested, charged, and found guilty for the murders of the Avery family. He died via lethal injection in 2006.

"We knew very well it could be either one of us, or someone of our family. No one really knew [who] was going to end up in that hole for sure."
    –Ron Luff, former cult member

Chapter Nine

In German, Hörst Du Das Means 'Do You Hear That?'

Hinterkaifeck, Germany. 1922

Maybe I shouldn't have come. The Hinterkaifeck farm-house is quiet until the little girl speaks to me. Her voice is like a scream in the silence. I almost cover my ears. So you're the new girl, she says to me, craning her little neck and inspecting my face for signs of something–I don't know what. She's trying to scare me.

Hast du Angst?

No, I'm not scared, I say. Then I ask, *of what*, thinking of it too late.

The last girl left us, the little girl says. She heard things above us at night. She told me that people walked around the ceiling while we slept. She said it was ghosts. Dead people, right?

I tell the little girl with brown braids on either side of her head that there are no such things as ghosts. The last girl was silly and they should be glad she's gone. We sit across from one another at the kitchen table while her Oma crochets in the next room. Suddenly, the old woman rises.

Hörst du das?

No, I tell Oma, I didn't hear anything. The little girl doesn't even look up as her Oma leaves out the backdoor, not putting on a winter coat but at least sticking her stocking-covered feet into heavy black boots.

The door shuts behind her, and the little girl leans forward as if to tell me a secret.

Ich habe es auch gehört.

When did you hear it? I ask her, and for some reason, I'm angry. I want to tell her to stop. She shrugs and tells me that sometimes, at night, she heard the walking. During the day, she thought she might have heard someone cough. Do ghosts get sick?

Opa found a newspaper, she says, and then she whispers and she sounds like a snake.

Wir bekommen die Zeitung nicht.

The postman dropped it, Opa said.

Aus München?

Yes, Opa said, the postman goes all over, even Munich. The little girl shakes her head and nearly smiles, but instead she clicks her tongue. She sounds so much like a little adult. The way a mother might say it. But not her mother, her mother is unusual, flighty.

Hörst du das?

No, I told Opa, I did not hear that. He says he thinks he hears Oma calling him. We're quiet and we strain to listen. Yes. There is something. Her older shaking voice comes in off the wind from outside.

Ich komme.

Opa gets up and rifles through the closet because Oma is wearing his boots. He finds a pair of shoes. The little girl tells her Opa that his socks will get wet, and she sounds almost sad. She almost looks at him as he leaves, with his hands in his pockets and his shoulders hunched against the cold, but she closes her eyes.

Wo ist Oma and Opa?

The little girl's Mutter comes from downstairs. She slept for most of the day. The little girl does not look at her Mutter, but she sighs when she enters the room. She tells her that Oma & Opa are in the barn. When her mother asks her why, she seems panicked, and I am not sure if this is how she always is. Always swarmed by emotion.

Schwärmerei.

There were tracks, says the little girl. She's only talking to me, she is ignoring her Mutter, but Mutter does not seem to notice. Mutter is only chewing on her lips and squeezing her hand with her fingers.

Groß.

How big? I ask the little girl. Mutter paces and paces, and then, finally, she lets out a sound that sounds almost like a sob.

She has to find them, Mutter says. Then she leaves. I did not see what she had on her feet. It made me nervous to look at her, afraid she might start shaking.

The little girl spreads her hands apart, this big, she says. They are bigger than a man's, I say.

Es ist wahr.

The little girl is upset now; she wants me to believe her, and I don't want to tell her that I do. But I do.

And last night, she says, looking up at the ceiling and cupping her hand over her mouth, last night, I heard them again. We all heard them. They laughed. They were eating. Ghosts don't eat, do they? She asks me, almost touching noses, and now her voice is trembling.

Hörst du das?

I tell her, no, I don't hear anything, but I am lying. I hear someone calling from outside. Many voices, going up and down with the wind.

Ich muss gehen.

No. Don't go, I tell her. But her boots are already on, small and brown and tied all the way up. Like she knew. Like she was waiting. She disappears out of the door, but she doesn't close it. I can see her slip in the snow as she walks, trying to move forward. The dark swallows her and the wind blows harder. I lie and say I cannot hear anything, and I'm covering my ears, but I can hear them all, and they are all screaming.

Sie kommen.

And I will wait.

In a Bavarian farm in 1922, six people were murdered with a grub axe, something you use to dig into the earth and cut roots with. Of the six murdered, five of them were related: Cazila Gruber, 72; Andreas Gruber, 63; Viktoria Gruber, 35; and Victoria's children, Cazilia, 7, and Josef, 2. Murdered alongside the family was their maid, Maria Baumgartner, 44. She was new. The previous maid had quit because she thought the house was haunted. She had heard things in the attic. Ghosts, maybe.

After the murders, it is speculated that the assailants stayed on the farm for a few days and even fed the animals.

"Viktoria Gruber, a 35-year-old widow, is said to have suddenly run into the woods the night before. It's not clear what made her do so, but reports say that there had been a "violent quarrel" leading up to it. Cäzilia followed her into the forest and found her crying hysterically."
–ALittleBitHuman.org

The case remains unsolved.

Chapter Ten

Moonlight Madness

Texarkana, AR. 1946

The town was behaving badly. June was reading about a maniac creeping in the dark on lover's lane, and she tried to remember where that was. Just below the headline was a pair of photos. The boy, Martin Reid, had terribly pronounced dimples that made him look cartoonish. His lips, spread out nice and wide, shined as if he had just licked them. The girl, Claire Booker, looked almost predatory in the picture next to his. She stared up at the camera through a fan of black eyelashes and smiled with dark lips. She was 16, but looked too old for her letter sweater. That name, Booker, was familiar somehow, but June couldn't place it.

"I wonder what he looks like now," June said, with her finger on Martin's picture.

"Or, I mean, just before."

"Probably not so good," Jimmy said.

Just three weeks before, another couple had been killed while they sat in their car in the dark, but the circumstances were a bit different. The man was almost 30, while the girl—really just a girl—was still in high school. People talked. Some details had been released in the papers. Their pockets had been turned out. The girl's parents didn't know the man. The man was married. The sheriff had even written a column in the Texarkana Star scolding his residents for gossiping, but people couldn't stop. They had worked themselves up and it felt like Texarkana was about to break open.

"Listen to this: 'Upon examination of the bodies, it is believed that they both fought very hard for their lives.'"

"I think Gracie is crying upstairs," Jimmy said.

"Oh, shoot, she's so quiet," June said.

"Do you want me to get her?"

"No, no, she's hungry I bet."

June walked up the stairs slowly. She was still thinking about Martin Reid's dimples as she padded into the room where the baby was red-faced and squirming desperately. The room was hot and smelled like a mixture of breast milk and unspoiled sweat.

She picked up the baby and held her to her chest. Gracie's lips were already puckering and her tongue darted in and out of her mouth. She had a small bump on her head, just behind her ear. A cyst, that's what the doctor told her it was. Jimmy had one right at the top of his head, but you couldn't see it unless he got his hair wet. His shark fin, he said. Her hair would eventually cover it up, too, but June loved it. It was the only proof that

Gracie belonged to the both of them, because otherwise she was all June. The baby's eyes had already started to turn hazel, and her new tufts of hair were coming in brown.

June felt a flash of panic when she started bouncing her. Gracie was so small still—again, perfectly normal is what the doctor said. June almost couldn't bear how fragile her baby was. If she just held her tighter, she could constrict her like a snake. Tighter still and she pictured her breaking into a million tiny pieces—like a milk jug shattering on the ground. She closed her eyes and shook her head from side to side. "No," came out of her mouth without her noticing.

"Everything okay?" Jimmy called from downstairs.

She nodded to Gracie and unbuttoned her shirt.

***

June stood at the front door staring at the lock.

"Jimmy, can you run to the store and get a deadbolt? Get two—one for the front and back."

"Oh, we're fine, June. Our locks are good, I just put new knobs on them a few months ago. Remember?"

"Please, it makes me nervous," June said.

"It's not happening to people in houses," Jimmy said.

He put an arm around her but June shrugged him off. The first man was older than them.

"I don't care, Jimmy. I want the locks. We don't know what'll happen next, we don't know anything, and no one's been caught. I just think about Gracie and it feels like I can't breathe.

What if something happens to us and she's all alone? Who would take care of her? Her grandparents are too old and your sister's a mess . . ." Her voice was rising in volume.

"Hey, baby. You need to calm down. I'll go to the hardware store and get the locks. It's okay. Everything is okay."

"Will you get them today?"

"I'll go after I stop by work, before my poker game, how does that sound?"

"Okay," June said.

June glanced back at the door.

"I think I'm just tired. I haven't been getting much sleep. It's hard to sleep in the middle of the day. It's too bright," June said.

"Why don't you try, I'll go close the curtains and turn on the fan."

"Can we go now?" June asked.

"Upstairs?"

"To the hardware store."

"Jesus, June."

"Please, let's just get it done? It'll help me sleep."

***

The streets were emptied out. In that heat, people usually poured outside of their homes and ran their hoses. It was a terribly bright day and the sunlight bounced off the pavement so hard it made June squint. The cicadas were making a high-pitched ringing sound and it seemed like everything was about to burst.

Only two people were working at Cole's hardware; Houston Cole Senior and Houston Cole Junior. Junior had some sort of defect. He either had something missing or had too much of something else, is what Jimmy used to say in high school. Hunched over and rail thin, he kept both of his hands in his pockets, or else he would be playing with them while he avoided looking at whoever he was talking to.

"I think he did it," Jimmy whispered in June's ear as they walked down the aisles.

"Be quiet," she said as she covered up a laugh.

"All these fluorescents are making him ghostly."

"Hush, he'll hear you," she said.

"Good, he'll know we're onto him and leave us alone."

"Or he'll come get us."

"If it's Junior Cole, I think I like my chances."

"You think you can take him?"

"That hurts, your own husband." He put his hand on his chest and stumbled back.

"Can I help you find anything?"

June jumped and started laughing. Jimmy straightened up and began tripping over his words.

"Where'd you come from, Jesus you scared the hell out of me," Jimmy said.

"I didn't mean to."

"Houston, we're looking for some deadbolts—you know, for doors," June said.

"Sorry, ma'am. We're all out of locks. Dad put in for another shipment but they won't be in until next week."

Jimmy grabbed at the back of his own neck and squeezed. "Ah, shoot. You sure about that? With everything going on, we were looking for the extra protection." Jimmy danced around that last word, as if the mere mention of it exposed a lack.

"Seems that's what everyone's after right now."

"Sure, okay."

"We have some firearms in aisle eight, I could show you those if you wanted?"

"No," Jimmy said. "I got a Winchester back at home."

"Thank you, Junior," June said.

"But we're almost out of those, too—that's another thing people seem to be buying a lot of. So if you change your mind, we might not have them."

"We're okay," June said.

"Did you know that girl?" Junior asked.

Gracie started crying—little squeak noises, nothing too loud, she was never too loud. It always made June nervous that she was missing the sound at night, so she would keep herself absolutely still and breathe shallow, waiting for that small crack in the silence.

"What girl?" Jimmy asked, lowering his voice.

"The dead girl. The one in the car?"

The two looked at each other. Houston still hadn't looked up from the ground.

"No, Junior. Did you know her?"

"Her mom, Mrs. Booker, came in here and ordered things for the house. She was painting the kitchen—Canary yellow, number 303. She lives at 4151 Ivy Lane. Two and a half blocks away from your house, you see?"

Suddenly Cole Senior appeared behind his son. He put one of his rough, large hands on Junior's shoulder and Junior stood stock-still.

"This boy here has a knack for remembering phone numbers, addresses, orders. Why, I could go without keeping a record of things around here, of course I don't, but I wouldn't have to if I didn't want to. It's all right up here." He pointed to the top of his son's head. "Go ahead, ask him where anyone lives Texas side, go on, just think of anybody that comes to mind."

June rocked Gracie, who was stretching her fingers in and out of a tiny fist. Jimmy said they had to get going but they'd be back next week, and it would be great if they could put aside some deadbolts for them.

"Mrs. Booker," June said. "From Texas High?"

"Yes, mhm," Junior hummed.

Mrs. Booker landed June with a "C" instead of an "A" because she hadn't put her name on her paper. Written across the top in bright red was only a line of question marks, one after the other, in varying sizes. It was the first "C" that June had ever gotten, and she blamed that woman for every one that followed.

Jimmy put his hand on her back and began pushing her away.

"I think a lot of folks knew Claire, I think because everyone who comes in here is talking about her. I haven't heard much about Martin, the boy, but a lot of people are talking about Claire; how it happened in the car," Junior said.

"Thanks, Junior. We'll see you," said Jimmy

"We'll see you soon," said Senior.

They started walking down the aisle towards the door when June turned back.

"Where did you say Mrs. Booker lived again?"

Senior's brow furrowed and he looked to his son. Junior recited it over, clear as day—no mumbling. He looked up from his feet, making eye contact for the first time with a smile on his face. He did love to show off.

***

Five cars parked outside the house on Ivy Lane. The screened-in porch contained dozens of potted Calla Lilies. The ribbons tied around the flower baskets were in pastel colors, pinks, yellows, and blues, like it was Easter Sunday. June leaned forward in her seat as Jimmy shifted anxiously next to her.

"We should do something."

"Like what?" His eyes focused on the rearview mirror in case anyone might pull up behind them.

"I could bring her over some food?"

"We don't know her."

"Sure we do, besides, we're neighbors; it'd be kind of us."

"We're not neighbors, June. We never come this way."

"Still."

"You can do what you want, but I'd rather not interrupt this woman's grief with introductions."

"It wouldn't be like that."

"Sure it wouldn't." Jimmy pulled his car out without looking, nearly cutting off a car coming from the opposite direction. He winced when they honked, as if the sound had hurt him somehow.

***

June flipped through her cookbook as she stretched her legs over Jimmy's lap on the couch. He had kept trying to slide them off him, "It's too hot," he said. But she kept putting them back.

"I don't know what's appropriate; people usually do casseroles, I think. I've never done this before."

"Then maybe you shouldn't start."

"Just because you're mean, I don't have to be. We should show her that we're there for her. That the neighborhood is there for her."

"So you represent the neighborhood now? You barely know who lives next door."

"This is different—and we do know her, she was our English teacher."

"She won't remember us. Do you know how many kids go through Texas? And how many since us? It's been 10 years."

"You don't know, maybe she will."

"So what's your plan then? Are you going to walk up and ask her how it happened?"

She kicked him with her heel.

"Of course not. If she wants to talk I'll be there, that's all."

"Why would she want to talk to you, June? I don't like this. You're not like this, I don't know what's gotten into you, but I don't want you to do it—you can't."

"I can't?"

"No, I won't let you bother that woman."

Jimmy got up and walked out of the room and out the back door, slamming it behind him. June braced herself for the little noises from upstairs, but she didn't hear anything. After a few minutes of waiting she went up to check on Gracie. June looked down into the crib and found her opening and closing her tiny fists as she stared at the painted yellow stars on the ceiling, but not making a sound. June wondered if you could call that color canary.

***

She was behind. She had started making everything right after Jimmy had gone to work, and for a while it was going okay. The artichokes were boiling while Gracie wanted to eat, Gracie was napping while June cut up the chicken—things had been working out in a way that made her think this was supposed to happen. But then the timer and Gracie's appetite started to overlap. June could feel the tightness across her chest as she unbuttoned her dress. She had waited too long. Gracie took to it quickly and June buzzed. She needed to keep moving, to keep track and to keep checking. Her mind was turning over, too, so fast that before she knew it she had planned out the whole conversation with Mrs. Booker. What June would say, how she would embrace her—put a hand on her arm and then hold her, if she wanted that, which she would. Then June heard a noise come from her daughter. A kind of grunt that sounded like a question. Still in her lap, Gracie had stopped sucking, and stared at her mother with furrowed brows. The two held each other's gaze until the timer rang, a sound that cut right into the room. The food was burning and she had to start again.

June's eyes darted between the timer and the road; she was waiting for Jimmy to pull up in his truck, and the bell rang as he turned onto the road. The sun bounced off the hood into the house. She grabbed the food out of the oven and thought about hiding it in one of the cupboards, but it was still too hot so she ran out the backdoor and behind the shed that they never used. She set it down in the dirt and walked back, following the trail of food she had spilled on the way out.

"Where did you come from?" Jimmy asked.

"Just needed some fresh air. It got a little smoky in here—I burned dinner."

"That's too bad—you okay? You're sweating."

"I spilled everywhere."

June stuck a rag under the faucet and the sink made a moaning sound as water sputtered out. She jumped and then she started to laugh.

"I don't know what's wrong with me."

"Listen, I'm sorry about this morning. Everyone's been on it at work and it makes me sick the way they all talk about it. It's not our business."

"It's not some town secret, though. People were murdered, Jimmy. In pairs. We're not even safe when we're together. Everybody's terrified."

"That's not what I mean," he said.

"What do you mean, then? How should people react? Pretend like there's no one out there? Leave our doors wide open? Invite the guy in for dinner?"

"The way he talked was disrespectful. To them. That's what I mean. He was acting like a peeping tom."

June stood there wringing her hands together. She understood. She wasn't like that, though. It wouldn't be like that.

"Besides, I doubt he eats at the same time as the rest of us, and what would we make him?" He looked at her with just one corner of his mouth turned up.

"You're awful."

"What happened here?" He tugged on her dress.

"I got it all over. I should go take this off."

Jimmy brought the skirt all the way up to his face and smelled it.

"Hey, what are you doing?" she laughed, pulling away just a little.

"I want to know what you made. What is that? Smells like some sort of bird? Absolutely, that's what it is. Let me get closer."

June leaned against the sink for balance, smiling, as Jimmy fell to his knees on the floor, holding onto her legs.

"Now tell me, does it fly?"

"Does what fly?"

"The bird, does it fly?"

"What a strange question, all birds fly."

"Not true, June. Not true. Some birds—like penguins, they don't fly," he said, sliding his hands up her legs.

"I didn't burn any penguins. This bird could fly—but not too well."

***

June watched Jimmy walk down the street to his weekly poker game. He left the house hungry, with his hands in his pockets, and walked as though nothing was holding him to the earth. She imagined him whistling, even though he never got the hang of it. She used to tease him by cat-calling. "One of us should be able to do it," she'd say as they passed each other in the halls at school. Sometimes he'd try but it came out in nothing but air. When he had turned the corner June ran back outside. The chicken casserole was still mostly intact. She grabbed Gracie and the food and walked out the front door.

The sun was setting and it was still hot. Gracie's body was making an imprint of sweat on her dress, but she was still sleeping. Like Jimmy, she sweat buckets in her sleep—no matter how much or little she was dressed. June had gotten good at balancing two, or three, or four things at once. Gracie and a book. Gracie and the newspaper. Gracie and a glass of milk. June's arms were strong, but she could feel the left one start to quiver as she held on to the casserole. There weren't any cars out front that night. She walked up the lawn and got herself into the screened porch without letting the door bang shut behind her, and she very suddenly felt like an intruder. It was a dirty feeling, and she was relieved when she saw all the lights off. Mrs. Booker wasn't home, then. June could just set it on the porch and go—she wouldn't even leave a note. She was at the door with the dish in her hands when she saw the woman inside.

Mrs. Booker was sitting in a chair facing the windows. She sat in the dark staring straight ahead. She should have been able to see June outside, but it didn't feel like she was seeing anything at all. She could have been sleeping with her eyes open. Mrs.

Booker's dress was bunched around her and it seemed that she had missed a button or two. Behind her there were photos of Claire on the wall. At least 10 of them arranged chronologically in rows. The first was a faded baby photo, but Claire's dark eyes were still clear and wet looking, as if the photographer had just gotten her to stop crying. At the end of the line was an empty spot on the wall, a square that was almost burnt into the wallpaper with a single hook sticking out of the middle. One was missing.

Gracie started to cry and June dropped the dish. It shattered and she ran. She made it half way down the block before she heard someone call after her.

"Wait!" Mrs. Booker yelled. "Just wait!"

June stopped and turned around. Mrs. Booker was walking up to her slowly, her dress looking even more awkward and uncomfortable, like it was two sizes too small. Mrs. Booker was finally to her, and June hadn't moved any closer.

"Do I know you?"

"I'm so sorry," June said.

"Did you know Claire?"

"I didn't mean to bother you. I'll clean it up, I just need to put my baby down."

"She sounds hungry, I know that sound." Mrs. Booker stepped closer reaching her hand out and stroking Gracie's head; her fingers found the bump behind her ear and she traced a circle around it. "May I?"

June handed her over like an offering, and Mrs. Booker took her, carefully cradling her head. While her former teacher's appearance hadn't changed in 10 years, there was nothing of the woman that June had remembered. There was no edge, no sharpness. She was just a mother. It seemed she never could have been a teacher, or a child, or anything else at all.

They walked back to the house while Mrs. Booker cooed the baby, bouncing her a little, up and down. She opened her front door. Without taking her eyes off Gracie, Mrs. Booker told June that the towels were in the kitchen and there was a small trashcan near the sink. June went in as Mrs. Booker waited on the porch. The house was suffocating. None of the windows were open and there was a stale smell, like a person who had not bathed.

Mrs. Booker stood over her while she kneeled on the porch picking up the shards of glass. The moonlight came through the screens and lit up parts of Mrs. Booker's face. Silently she stared at the child, without moving at all.

"What's her name?"

"Grace, we call her Gracie."

"Why did you come here? Did you know my Claire?" she asked, not looking at her. Mrs. Booker didn't remember her, and that didn't matter.

"I didn't. My husband and I live close by, on Tulip over there." She pointed in the wrong direction.

"I didn't know I had so many neighbors. It was just Claire and me." Mrs. Booker brought her hand up and scratched at a spot on her neck. June noticed a long scrape that looked raw and exposed. Mrs. Booker caught her staring.

"It's a bad habit. When I'm nervous I scratch. Claire hated it. She would pull my hand down whenever I started up, like when I tried to get her to stop biting her nails." Mrs. Booker looked at her own and smiled. "Well, as you can imagine, this has been a bad week to quit any vices." She tried to laugh but it came out like a soft and uneven humming sound.

"She was a real boss. You know, she even had a job. Played her sax for Gus and the High Notes—she was a high note. She was playing that night, before—they can't find her saxophone." Mrs. Booker started to scratch. "I waited, you know? I always waited. She'd come home and no matter how late we'd talk, she'd tell me everything, from what she played to what she ate. She told me everything. I would sit and smile. The way she talked about the people in the crowd sounded like she was telling me about a movie. Who danced. Who sat. Newcomers. Regulars. People who had too much. It was all so important to her. Every detail." Then Mrs. Booker turned to Gracie. "I just—well, I just worshiped her."

Gracie started to squirm. June finished and stood up, wiping the hair off her forehead.

"Oh my. I didn't notice before, but you're leaking," Mrs. Booker said.

June could only think of when her water broke. Mrs. Booker handed Gracie back and June felt the dampness of her dress press against her chest. There was a name stenciled just above Mrs. Booker's left breast. In the moonlight she could see the cursive stitching—"Claire" was written over the place where her mother's heart had continued to beat.

***

June walked home with Gracie asleep against her chest. Her shoes were in her other hand because she had a piece of glass stuck in the arch of her foot. She was walking awkwardly, on the edge of her feet, and it was almost like dancing. June gazed at her daughter and the last pieces of her baby blonde hair were soaking in moonlight. She wanted Gracie's hair to hold onto it, like the way it gets brighter in the summertime. If she pressed her face against her baby's head she wanted it to smell like night, but she didn't do that. She wanted her to sleep now.

June walked up the front porch steps, leaving a bloody footprint on every other one. The front door to her house was stuck when she twisted the knob. It would turn to either side, but she couldn't get it open so she shook it a little more. Her arms were tired and she was having a hard time balancing Gracie on her chest so she set her down gently on the porch. June wrapped both her hands around the doorknob and started to tug at it, spreading her feet apart for leverage, bearing down on the sliver—and then it happened fast. In the window next to the door she saw her red and white curtains shake and there was a man there she had never seen before, but she knew exactly who he was. Jimmy stared back, and his eyes were glassy and wide enough that she thought she could see all the white in them. His skin seemed drained of Texas sun, leaving him pale, almost sickly looking. He pressed his Winchester tightly to his chest, and, for just a moment, she thought she saw him pulling the rifle down, leveling it between the curtains, as though she, too, were unrecognizable. She thought, in that moment, that she might have scared him to death. Gracie started screaming.

In Texarkana, AR, over the span of three months in 1946, five people were murdered and others attacked as a serial killer targeted couples in cars on lovers' lanes. The town went into a panic as the attacks continued unsolved. It inspired one of the first slasher films.

"Texarkana looked normal during the daylight hours. But everyone dreaded sundown . . ."
–*From* The Town that Dreaded Sundown

Chapter Eleven

Mom & Dad's Bed

San Bernardino, CA. 1964

There are pictures I've seen of my parents, but they don't look like my parents. They are young, but it's more than that. They are together and they are touching and the expressions they are making are pulling their faces into contortions that aren't natural for them. Almost like there was a mistake with the printing process. Their smiles are so large that I can see the black gaps between the insides of their cheeks and their teeth. Too big. These pictures are tucked away in old photo albums that are themselves tucked away in the back corners of unchecked china cabinets. We stopped using china after my third brother was born. I didn't even know these albums existed.

When my mother asks me to get them, I'm nervous about reaching my hand into the dark. I thought I would smell smoke and then another black burned hand would wrap around my wrist. I would see white wet eyes staring back at me. My father's eyes.

"Get what?"

"The pictures, we need them for the boards," my mother says with her cigarette between her pink, chapped lips. I saw little pieces of dry skin all caked up with lipstick. "Pull out all the photo albums from the china cabinet." She doesn't look at me when she's giving me these instructions, she is making her bed, and I leave her in there alone. Maybe she needs a moment in the space they shared.

Maybe, then, she'll cry for him.

There are four albums. I thought one for each kid, but Tommy was born just two years before and I can't remember taking a single picture with him around. Maybe this woman looks a little like my mother. I remember a smile like that, but it's fading. Like something I could have dreamt years ago—how people still remember certain nightmares, or the way their baby blanket smelled in the dark. I look up at my mother as she vibrates around the house, I want to compare the two women.

"Mom," I say, and she whips around like a ballet dancer, turning perfectly on her toes. I could see the pronounced arches on her feet from where I sat in the dining room. They were something she used to brag about. Her father, a doctor, had put her in orthopedic shoes the moment she started to walk.

"Yes," she says, and there it is. That smile. That big smile with gaps and teeth that reached all the way up to her eyes. There were lines around her eyes now, but she looked just like the woman in the photo. My mother. It made me nervous.

There is a picture of my father when he graduated from med school. He is standing between his mother and father with his graduation robes and cap tilted over his eye. He is smirking. That is a look I know. The slight turns of his lips, up or down, were familiar to me. His deep brown eyes that were nearly black, sunk into his face like stones, so the sum of it all was brooding. Like a young movie star. Arrogant, maybe. Or apathetic. I pull it out from behind the plastic film, peeling it off the sticky board pages and trying not to rip. I go slow.

There is a wedding photo and my father is not smirking. He's serious now, concentrating. My mother, though, is elated. She must have moved when the picture was taken because her edges, particularly her shoulders and hips, are blurred.

Did you love him? I want to ask her now, as she lays out a black dress on the ironing board in the living room, still constantly moving her body in some small way, blurring her edges. She was excited in the picture. She was excited now.

There are three birth photos. In the first, she is holding one baby and her face is shiny. She is tired but happy. My father is standing with one hand in his pocket and another on her shoulder. His eyes suggest contentment, but that is all I can tell. I am the baby, their first. Then there is the next. I am still there, I am sitting on my mother's lap as she holds Paul. I am looking down into his face. My mother is looking at my father who is not looking at anything because his eyes are closed. Then Ray. My mother's two older children are perched on a chair in the hospital room, awkwardly holding the baby across their laps like a loaf of bread they don't want to roll off and touch the floor. My mother took the picture but my father is not in it.

I remember her standing in front of us with the camera, her hospital gown strings dangling between her legs.

I remember that my father did not come. I remember them shouting.

"So I'll drive myself then? What kind of man are you?"

Or my mother shouting and my father not saying anything, like he couldn't hear her. He just stayed under the covers of their bed. He was sick, mom said. Sometimes he needed to rest.

On the next page, there is a picture of our trip to Hawaii. I remember this trip. I was seven, my brother was four, and my other brother was just a baby. Tommy hadn't been born. I am sitting on the bed in the hotel room with my mother who is wearing a short-sleeved men's button-down shirt over her swimsuit. I am squeezing her mouth between my fingers, trying to force it up into a smile. My brothers are tanned and shirtless on the floor, playing with a toy ship. My father is not in this picture, but I know he didn't take it. I had set the automatic timer and put the camera on the Formica topped dresser across the room with brass palm leaves for handles. I remember the flash. Flash. Flash.

I turn the page and find nothing. I look in the other three albums and find nothing. They are empty. Two still have the price sticker stuck to the back. Three dollars and fifty cents.

"It's time to go," my mother says, dressed with the boys surrounding her like little suited planets, circling and circling. She is holding my dress. It is also black, and shaped like hers. A mommy and daughter set she bought days ago. I tell her it's stiff, but she says it is only for today. After this we can burn it. Her choice of words is a mistake but she doesn't seem to realize.

In the funeral home, she sets the boards up in the lobby herself, my brothers holding them as she stretches out the stands. I have Tommy on my hip. He is playing with my hair. His eyes look like my father's, but nothing else is the same. His smile is gummy. I want to take a picture.

People start to come in, but not so many. My father did not have a lot of friends. His coworkers walk toward my mother who stands next to my father's closed casket. Because of the fire, it couldn't be open, but I still imagined what his face looked like now. Maybe his lips had burned away and he was showing that same exaggerated smile he had in the first pictures. Unnatural.

My mother keeps a hand on the edge of the casket when she is not talking to someone who is telling her they're sorry. She nods, smiles politely, twists the wedding ring on her finger before she hugs them or shakes their hand. I am tasked with keeping my brothers well-behaved. Paul won't stop playing with his tie—the tie he got from my father's closet. One I had never seen my father wear. Even though he was a doctor, he never dressed himself properly. Sloppy. Once I caught my mother trying to fix his collar, and he swatted her hand away like she was a bug. Later, after he left for work, she cried at the kitchen table and I watched.

Did you love him?

They found my father's car on fire on HWY 30. They told my mother in the doorway to our beige bi-level ranch that he was dead before the fire.

"How do you know?" My mother asked, her fingers pulling on her lip, her other hand pushing my brothers back into the house. I could tell that the question was inappropriate. It left something wrong in space between the officers on the front porch and all of us in the house. My mother knew, too. She started to close the door.

There is a man who approaches the casket that I've never seen. But he isn't looking at the casket, he is looking at my mother and he looks like he is in love. My mother smiles. A big smile with those dark gaps between her cheeks and her teeth.

"I'm so sorry," this strange man says. His skin is freckled and reddish—I can smell the sun on him.

"Thank you," my mother says, and she doesn't shake his hand or hug him. Instead, she pushes me forward.

"This is my daughter, Stephanie."

"You look just the same as your mom," the man says.

I tell him I have my father's smile, and my mother laughs. The man, not knowing what to do, not understanding, simply turns around and walks away. My mother pulls me closer and kisses my head. Again, I think I can smell the sun.

We leave the photo boards at the funeral home. My mother says we will get them later, but I know we won't.

"It's been a long day. Let's rest," my mother says. She invites us all into her bed. The bed she shared but didn't really share with my father. There was no trace of him there, no indentation, no sweat stains. It was almost as if he had barely existed. My mother tried to gather us all up in her arms, Tommy lying on her chest, the boys on either side of her, and our heads touching.

"Goodnight, my love," she says to me, and she turns out the lights. Suddenly, I am in the gap in her mouth as she smiles so big.

This story was loosely based on the Lucille Miller Case, a woman charged, convicted and imprisoned for the murder of her husband. She was paroled after seven years and appeal efforts lasted years.

Lucille Miller and Dr. Gordon "Cork" Miller were married for 15 years and had 4 children together. Throughout their marriage, Cork suffered from severe depression and expressed the desire to end his life on multiple occasions. In October of 1964, Lucille and Cork went out to buy milk at night in their VW Bug. According to Lucille, the tire popped and caused a fire and she wasn't able to get Cork out. According to the police, it was murder. Others have thought something closer to a mercy killing. Either way, for the rest of her life, she lived for her children.

"Ron, Guy and I all married, but never had children. We were hopelessly entangled with our mother until the day she died."
–Daughter, Debra Miller

The names in this story were changed to my siblings' names, as we were all hopelessly entangled with our own mother until the day she died. And she lived for us.

Chapter Twelve
Cabin 28
Keddie, CA. 1981

"I need you to check on my wife. I haven't heard from her."

"Sure, I'll put you through, sir."

"No, no, it's been six days, you've got to go—"

***

Jim, Sarah, and Deb parked the rental black Volkswagen Rabbit outside their cabin. Jim and Sarah sat in the front seat, and with his hand resting on his wife Sarah's thigh, Jim looked at Deb and winked.

"Well, this is nice. A little small. Maybe it's a good thing after all that Charlie couldn't get out of work," Sarah said. She was still looking out the windshield at the single-story yellow-painted log cabin, so Deb, feeling impulsive and darling and, yes, even a little sexy, snuck a smile to herself. Then she looked up through her half-opened eyes at Jim. He was still staring, and her stomach tightened when he licked his lips.

***

Ring.

   Ring.

   Ring. Ring. Ring. Ring. Ring. Ring. Ring. Ring. Ring. Ring. Ring. Ring. Ring.

   Ring.

   Ring.

   Ring.

"Fucking damnit," Charlie yelled to the empty air between rings. His stomach was tight.

***

"I'm so glad you could still come with us," Sarah said as the three of them walked in a single-file line through the front door. There were daisies painted up and down in vertical lines.

They held their suitcases and stood in the small living room with a dirty braided rug and two loveseats on either side. Set for conversation. No TV. A round cafe table sat by a window with white cotton curtains. Deb thought it was too much. Too quaint. Too lovely. They all took it in very quietly. Very still. Then, not realizing that the moment was reverent or something near sacred, Sarah moved, charging into the room toward the bedrooms—everything about her too loud.

152

Sarah opened one door, then another. They each had an acrylic-painted Sunflower. The yellow peeling at the edges of the petals. The chips and cracks obvious on the dark oak wood. There were flies making too much noise. They buzzed around in the corners of Deb's vision. Almost like she had something in her eye. Deb even touched the corners of her eyes with her finger, though she knew they were not on her.

"They're the same size. Full beds. Take your pick, Deb," Sarah said with a smile.

Deb took the one at the front of the house. A window overlooked the porch. She could see the car. If she needed to leave quietly, she thought.

"I'm starving," Jim said, and Deb wondered if he was saying it to one of the women in particular.

"I should call Charlie and let him know we made it," Deb said, staring at the mustard-colored phone on the wall in the kitchen. She had the distinct sensation, a premonition in her hand, in her right palm, that the receiver would burn her when she picked it up. Like a demon and holy water.

"Is he even home from work yet?" Jim asked. He asked it while he stretched his arms over his head. Trying too hard to be casual. As if Deb wouldn't notice he was trying to put more space between them here, and Charlie, who was not here. Still, Sarah nodded and agreed with her husband.

Deb shrugged. "I guess you're right. What time is it?"

"Time for a drink," Sarah said.

***

"Sunset Lodge, how can I help you?"

"Do not transfer me, you little shit," Charlie said.

"Sir?" Said the twenty-year-old Thomas with two pimples on either side of his large and shiny nose.

"This is the 10th time I've called. You keep transferring me, and no one has answered. I haven't spoken to my wife in six days. I don't know if the phone is broken or if I should be calling the police. Do you understand me?"

"Yes, sir," Thomas said, his heart sinking in his narrow chest.

"I want someone, maybe you, maybe someone who doesn't have shit for brains, to physically walk your ass over to my wife's cabin, knock on the door, and not leave until a Deborah Ann Fishly opens and says 'yes, I'll call my husband right away.'"

***

Jim handed Deb a drink while she sat on the rocking chair on the front porch. Sarah was inside making them dinner. Something with ground beef. Sarah was singing to herself. She wasn't looking. Jim put his hand on Deb's shoulder. His fingers were freezing and wet from the cocktail he made her that Deb already knew would be overly strong. He walked his fingers up her neck and then held her jaw in his hand—standing over her, making her see him.

"Jim," Deb said, but she didn't move—or try to move. He stared at her, then he glanced at something behind her, just over her shoulder.

"Keep your window open," he said.

"Bugs will get in," Deb said.

"Let them."

***

Thomas felt stupid. Like he'd just been yelled at by his drunk dad. Thomas saw the three of them come in on that first day. The one woman, who smiled too much, walked inside the main lodge while the other two waited outside. Thomas could see the other two, a man and a woman, and it was like they were trying not to try standing too close to each other. At least the woman was. She had short, curly brown hair. Like Thomas's mom, but she was younger. Maybe 30. Skinny. The man who stood next to her snaked his hand behind her back. Thomas watched as the tendons in the man's arm tensed. He pulled the other woman toward him, pressing his body against hers as the woman who was checking in said her name was Sarah Braucher, her husband, Jim Braucher, was outside with their friend Deb Fishly, and they had rented Cabin 28 for 10 days. Charlie Fishly was on the reservation, but he would not be staying.

"Oh," Thomas had said.

He felt bad for Sarah Braucher, then. But now, if the guy calling was the other woman's husband, he was glad. Charlie Fishly sounded like a real asshole.

***

They drank, the three of them. They had brought with them an inordinate and disproportionate amount of booze. Even if Charlie had come, this looked like enough for a bachelor party. Sarah drank the most. It was noticed by everyone, but no one more than Sarah herself, who kept repeating, each time she struggled getting off the loveseat, that she shouldn't have another, but they were on vacation.

Deb drank, but she was not drunk. She only wanted to calm her nerves because she was nervous. More than she expected. Jim, Deb realized after a few hours switching between talking about nothing and sitting in excruciating silence, only had one drink in his hand the whole time, and it was half full. The realization made Deb more nervous, and she had another drink.

***

Cabin 28 was the southernmost structure on the grounds. It was also the cheapest because it butted up against the highway, and you could hear the cars at night. Thomas thought about taking the golf cart, but then decided to walk. When he thinks back on this decision, years from this day, he still doesn't know why he made it. He can't remember, but it is because, just then, he wanted to make that asshole wait.

***

"I don't feel good," Sarah said slowly, trying very hard to get the words to sound right. She leaned over her knees, and then she threw up, like a child, all over the braided rug.

"Oh, jeez," Jim said, before casually taking a sip of his drink.

Deb waited a moment, watching Sarah's shoulders roll and her dyed blonde hair fall in her face, before she understood that Jim wasn't going to do anything.

"Here," Deb said, moving quickly to Sarah's side.

"Sorry," Sarah said before throwing up again. "I'll clean this tomorrow, please don't touch it."

Deb swept Sarah's hair up, and one lock, that was coated with vomit, slid between her fingers.

"Jesus," Deb said, letting all the hair go and rubbing her hand on her shorts.

"Sorry," Sarah said, again.

"Let's go to the bathroom," Deb said, grabbing Sarah's arm with the same hand that had touched the vomit. Deb grabbed Sarah's arm hard.

***

The car was there. The VW Rabbit was in the same spot it had been since they got there. Thomas knew that because it had rained and there were no tire tracks in the mud. The rain had erased the ones they made coming in. Like nature itself was covering up for these people. But there were other tracks. Large footprints. It looked like they walked to the cabin and then away. Back and forth. Back and forth.

***

Deb turned on the shower and helped Sarah out of her clothes.

"It's cold," Sarah said.

"It will warm up. Just give it a minute. Let's get this out of your hair."

Sarah pushed Deb's hands off, tilting away from her but not falling, thankfully. "Don't touch him," Sarah said.

"What?" Deb asked, her skin began to crawl and shiver.

"Me. Don't touch me. I can do it myself," Sarah said. Then she threw up again.

***

The absence of noise. The absence of any noise at all. It was starkly quiet at Cabin 28 in a way that it wasn't twenty yards back, or twenty yards ahead. A car went by on the highway that Thomas could see through the trees. The song coming out of the open windows, something by CCR, curled up and died when it reached the cabin. Swallowed by nothing. Thomas thought about calling out. Maybe they were on a hike or walked down to the river. But he knew that wasn't true. He had to knock on the door. But something about the painted daisies running up and down the front door made it look more like bars meant to keep him out or whatever inside, in.

***

Deb put Sarah in bed. She rolled the stiff quilt up over Sarah's shoulders. Jim walked aimlessly around the kitchen and living room. He wasn't quite pretending he was busy; it seemed like he was making it known that he was bored.

"Okay?" Deb asked.

Sarah nodded and turned onto her side, away from Deb. Deb thought she should get a bucket. There might be one outside. Sarah was still awake, she knew. Deb wondered if asking if she needed anything would set her off, again. If Sarah was now fortified with enough alcohol and humiliation to confront Deb about all of it. But just Deb. Not Jim. Deb guessed that Sarah knew there was no point in talking to Jim. About anything.

Deb left her. She walked across the living room and out the front door. She imagined Jim trying to stop her, misunderstanding what she was doing and reaching a hand out, but he just watched. On the front porch, in the corner, was a large white plastic bucket. It was filled with dead leaves and mucky water. Deb emptied it over the porch railing, and the sound the slop made as it sank into the earth continued somehow, even after the last drop left the bucket. She didn't understand. A rustling of the earth. Then something moved. She didn't see it, she sensed it, with her shoulders and the top of her head. Something came forward from the trees. She saw it, then, and she realized, with relief, that it was a car coming down the Lodge road. It was only that the headlights were off. And the car moved so slow. It started to rain.

***

Thomas was wrong. There was a sound. A loud kind of static that could be mistaken for nothing, at first. Something so loud that it filled the air and pushed out anything else, and you could be forgiven for thinking it was just air, or deafening silence, or you were having some kind of catastrophic medical event, and the first to go was your hearing. A flood. That's what it was. Thomas walked up to the door and knocked, and that sound that wasn't a real sound got louder.

***

Deb went to bed. She was still in her clothes. Her jean shorts and striped shirt now smelled like sweat and vomit. She lay on top of the covers. She knew she wouldn't have to wait long. Deb watched the open window. She heard flies and mosquitoes buzzing uncomfortably close to her ears, but still, she did not move. Instead of using the window, he came right through the door.

"She's dead asleep," Jim said as he shut the door quietly. Which was confusing because he had just spoken at a normal volume. He was not trying to be discreet. He sat down on the bed next to her, putting his hands on her chest. In the dark, she felt like she was waking up from a night terror, and the dark figure she saw sometimes was over her. Pressing down on her.

Not letting her move. Then Jim kissed her with his dry lips and struggled his tongue into her mouth.

***

"Hello?" Thomas yelled. He knocked again, and there was nothing. He stepped back and saw those same large footprints, the impression of a big man's shoe in dried mud there. And there. And there. Right up to the window. The open window. That was the noise. Flies, hundreds going in and out of the open window.

***

Deb stayed quiet until she heard a noise just outside the window. Like walking.

"What's that?" She asked, whispering.

Jim only continued to thrust, his hands grabbing and pinching her skin.

***

Thomas didn't understand what he saw. Not at first. It was a black cloud of flies in the room, crawling and covering things that suggested patterns he understood, but his brain kept rejecting as not quite right. Not quite whole. A hand. Curly brown hair infested with movement. Khaki pants bunched in the corner, untouched. Those he understood completely. Jean shorts wrapped around an ankle wrapped in mottled skin.

***

"Jim, stop. There's something." Deb began to push him off.

"It's an animal, we're in the woods. I'm close, baby, come on."

Darkness blocked out the window, then darkness started to crawl in, one leg at a time. His feet covered in mud. Like she always suspected, the terrors were real.

***

There was vomit on the rug. That's the first thing Thomas told his boss. Again, this is something he would never understand. When he got older, how he communicated what he saw. First, he talked about the vomit. Then he talked about the woman in her bed. The one who checked in. She was on her side. Her back was split open. Almost like an exoskeleton that had been emptied and broken. But it was not empty. Thomas could see parts of her that no one was supposed to see. She was facing the wall, but her face was covered with the blanket, like she had held it to hide underneath, but hadn't gotten it all over her in time—another thing he said to his boss while he cried, like a child, unaware that he was crying. The man was facedown in the other room. His arms underneath his body. The other woman was everywhere.

And somewhere else, not there, Charlie waited to hear from his wife. He thought he might throw up.

After separating from her husband, Sue Sharp and her five children moved across the country to live in a small cabin in northern California. In 1981, Sue, two of her children, and one of her children's friends were discovered murdered by daughter Sheila Sharp. They were murdered with knives and hammers and found bound with electrical tape and cords. The quadruple homicide has never been solved. This story is very loosely based on theirs.

"Although someone had covered the body of the mother with a blanket, it did little to relieve the horrific scene the teen and law enforcement encountered."
–Plumas County News

Chapter Thirteen

Undark

Ottawa, IL. 1930

Annie carefully handled the watch faces. Looking at them for ten hours a day could make it seem as if she dealt in frozen time. When she finally glanced up at the clock on the wall, she couldn't help but think it was strange when the hands moved. She had become more comfortable with time when it was stopped. She dipped the brush in the glow paint and did one slow stroke along the minute hand. Then she put the brush between her lips to gather the bristles to a point, and painted the stubby hour hand. She had to apply a certain amount of pressure without any assisting resistance, which was always difficult.

"I'm so tired, I could fall asleep with my eyes open," Vikki said.

"Mhmm," Annie hummed in an effort to keep her lips taut.

They had two hours left in the day, which would go slower the closer it came to an end. Of course, every job was like that, but the factory acted as a vacuum for time. Inside they kept the lights lower in order to better see the paint. The work was monotonous, but needed a steady hand and an eye for detail. Small, small details. The women—all of them were women—talked to each other but they did so quietly, fearing if they made louder noises it might knock their strokes out of line.

Vikki had been slowing down, lately. Her bin was coming up shorter and Annie would give her some to meet the quota. She slumped next to Annie, and her spine curved out from her dramatically, folding her down to the table. Annie tried to straighten herself out in response, trying to press herself up for as long as she could until she forgot. She always had fine posture. Years of her mother prodding with boney fingers at the middle of her back, or pulling at her shoulders, ensured it.

Unconsciously, she must have been mimicking Vikki, the way couples start to look like one another after a while because they pick up each other's mannerisms. Or how some people's dogs start to look like them. She hated the idea that Vikki might have more of an imprint on her than Frank, but it made sense. Annie had counted it out once. One-hundred-and-sixty-eight hours in a week and the saying went, "eight hours for work, eight hours for sleep, and eight hours for what we will." It would be nice if time split so perfectly, but Frank worked third shift at the glass plant. He slept until dinner, and Annie hesitated to call his first hour waking, but she needed the time so it would be four hours until he left at 10:30 p.m. Then she slept alone. She didn't even need the waking distinction, she spent more time with Vikki without question.

"I need a new brush," Vikki said, holding the pulled-out bristles in-between her teeth.

Annie reached for the jar of fresh ones, her fingers aching as she stretched them out for the first time in hours. She picked one out and handed it over without looking, but Vikki didn't grab it. She waited, pushing it closer, and still nothing.

"Here," she said.

But Vikki stared down into her own hand, in which she held something small. Annie leaned closer, rocking on her tailbone. It was a tooth. Not a piece of one, but whole. Wet and with roots, it shined in Vikki's hand like a pearl.

For a moment, Annie got the sensation that she was dreaming. She had never seen a whole adult tooth apart from the body, before. She had always taken care of her teeth. She looked up at Vikki who still studied it. Vikki swept a finger in her mouth and it came out with very little blood.

"I don't know," Vikki started.

"Let's go to the bathroom," Annie said.

She got up, grabbing Vikki's other hand so she could continue cradling the tooth. They walked to the bathroom, Annie trying to go as fast as she could so no one would see. Inside the pale small room, she had her sit down on the toilet.

"Open," Annie said.

Vikki shook her head.

"Come on, now. Let's see what happened."

"Nothing happened," Vikki said. It came out strange as she tried not moving her lips, like a ventriloquist.

"You must have bit on the brush, that's why the bristles came off."

She shook her head again and started to cry. Annie kneeled in front of her, folding her fingers over the tooth so she couldn't look anymore.

"It's just a tooth, dear. Let me see."

Vikki let out shaky breaths and opened her mouth a little. Annie could barely see, but she found the dark spot.

"It's a back tooth, you'll hardly be able to notice," she said.

Then she saw another blank space on the other side.

"Vikki," she said.

Vikki closed her mouth, rolling her lips in, making a straight, colorless line in her face, and shook her head as she started to cry. She brought her hands up to cover her face, but then the tooth was there.

"I don't know what's happening. Two this week. I thought it was an accident the first time. I was eating and maybe I had bitten down wrong. I thought it was strange that the whole tooth came loose, but I have had a terrible ache. I thought, just a cavity." She shrugged, her hands starting to shake.

"Did you make an appointment with the dentist?"

"I thought, since the tooth fell out, that I didn't need to anymore."

"What about the toothache? Still there?"

"It's everywhere." Vikki put her fingers to her jaw, but held them just over the skin, afraid to touch.

"Let's go after work, okay? I'll walk with you."

Vikki nodded, rubbing the tooth in her hand with her thumb.

***

The dentist was closed when they arrived, which is what Annie suspected would happen. Vikki stayed behind as Annie went up to the window and peered into the dark office. The hard dentist chairs and trays were reflecting some light from outside, but it was otherwise empty. She walked Vikki home. She only lived a few blocks from the factory. Vikki stayed quiet the whole way and stared down at the sidewalk. When they got to her door, Annie noticed that the white paint was chipping off, and the frame was slightly warped. Vikki went in, leaving the door open behind her, so Annie followed. The inside was dirty more than messy. It smelled like the inside of an unwashed laundry hamper. Vikki kept walking toward the back of the house without turning any lights on. She went into her bedroom and laid down, facing away from the door.

"Do you need anything?" Annie asked.

"I just need to rest, I'm so tired."

"Do you still have the tooth?"

Vikki stretched her arm behind her and opened up her hand, giving it to her. Annie hesitated and held her breath as she grabbed it.

"Where should I put it?"

"Next to the other one on my nightstand, there."

The other looked just like the one she held. For some reason, it surprised her. She laid it down so it would line up next to its twin.

"You'll go tomorrow morning, then? First thing?"

Vikki nodded with her head against the pillow. Her brown hair falling out of the bun it had been in.

"Do you want anything to eat before . . ." But she trailed off.

Vikki didn't answer.

"I'll come check on you tomorrow, after work. I'm sure it's nothing, darling. I'm sure you have nothing to be worried about. Could just be your diet, that's all."

As Annie struggled to shut the front door, she thought about what it might take to jam a tooth back into its place.

***

Frank was asleep in his chair when Annie walked in. The darkness in her house made her think a layer of grime was covering every surface, so she hurried over to the lamp that stood just over his head.

"God, Annie," Frank said, covering his face with both arms.

He barely opened his eyes as he looked up at her, trying to make her out in those first moments after waking. After he focused, he grabbed her hand and pulled her down onto his lap.

"Let's sleep a bit longer here, okay?"

She pressed into him for a moment, putting her face against his neck and smelling him before pushing herself off.

"I have to make dinner."

"Who can eat when they're this tired?"

"When *you* are tired. Besides, you have to work soon," she said as she walked into the kitchen.

"What time is it?"

"About 8:30."

"And you're just getting home? Where've you been?"

"Vikki's tooth fell out. Her second tooth, I guess, so I took over to the dentist, which was closed, then I walked her home," Annie said. "Oh, don't look like that, it's not what you think."

"What is it?" He said, dropping his hand from his mouth.

"I don't know, really. They weren't rotted, they looked like perfectly fine teeth."

Frank shivered. "I'm not so sure I'm ready to eat, just yet."

"You'll get over it."

"Well, I thought we might go lie down for a bit." He came up behind her, putting his hands on both of her arms and squeezing, just slightly.

She tried not to, but tensed against him, and he let go as if she had burned him.

"Nothing will happen if we don't try," he said as he walked back into the living room.

She grabbed hold of the counter and leaned over the sink. Her right hand still felt stiff from the day and she stretched it out. Annie turned on the faucet and splashed some cold water on her face. Thinking about going to bed with Frank terrified her. It had been months since it had been pleasurable. Months since they talked to each other quietly in their own home, as if they were teenagers. Months since they touched each other discreetly, and then luridly, with the freedom of not having to be careful. A different kind of fun than before. After the first twelve months, the first twelve disappointments of reaching down and finding that she had not stopped herself, they went to the doctor who told them, "Nothing to worry about. Sometimes it just takes a while. People always think it'll be easy, like they can think themselves into having a baby, but it can take work. All good things take work." The way he said it made it feel as if she was being scolded for being presumptive, or lazy. She tried to explain her family history, how her mother had eight children, and how Frank was one of ten, that it didn't seem to be an issue for any of her siblings. The doctor waved them off. After that, she dreaded sex. She started to see it as something she had to do until they got what they wanted, and then they could stop.

Frank had his head in his hands, and for a second Annie thought he was crying.

"Frank?" she asked.

He looked up at her, dry-eyed and angry.

"I'm sorry," she said. "I think it's me. I don't think I can."

Frank got up and put his arms around her. She thought, then, that it would be appropriate to cry, but she couldn't force herself to. She had gotten used to the feeling of being empty there. She thought of a dark cavity that was slowly spreading, but remembered that Vikki's teeth were almost perfectly white. Frank moved his hands and over her back, slowly. He sighed and hummed lowly against her hair. Now would be a good time to do something. To sway slightly against him, not seductively, but enough to respond. She couldn't, though. The rigidness ran through her, set deep in her bones, and she couldn't let it go. She tried, she imagined it leaking out and breaking apart in her blood. But, when she shifted, it was there still. Frank let go.

"Alright, Annie."

"I'm sorry."

"I have to go. They want me in early, tonight."

"What about dinner?"

"Not hungry," he said as he grabbed his coat and left.

Annie expected him to slam the door, but he didn't. He closed it as if he were trying to keep quiet.

***

Annie sat alone at work the next day, possibly for the first time. She couldn't remember a day before when Vikki wasn't there on her right. The longer the day went on, the more exposed she felt. Annie couldn't help herself from checking the clock on the wall, over and over, and it kept going, but slowly. She had never seen it go so slow. When she looked down at the watch face, only the fifth one she'd been able to put in her hand that day, her fingers tingled slightly, or she thought they did. She rubbed them on her skirt hoping the feeling would show itself again, but it didn't. Against her, her fingers felt normal.

"Are you alright?" The shift supervisor stood above her with her hands behind her back.

"I'm fine, sorry."

The supervisor tilted her head towards the empty bin.

"I know. I'm sorry, I haven't felt very well this morning."

"Ah, must be going around. Your table partner is ill as well."

"Did you talk to her?"

"No, somebody called on her behalf. I believe it was her doctor."

Annie looked over at the empty stool.

"Do you need to go home? I don't want anyone else on my floor getting sick."

"I think I might."

The woman smiled in a way that made Annie feel ashamed. She was thick all the way through. Not large, just solid. Sturdy. Someone had once said that about Annie, she couldn't remember who, maybe her father or an uncle, but it was a long time ago. The woman turned and stepped over to the next table. Annie put the watch face down. She had only painted the hands and half of the numbers. Three to nine. The dot in-between the five and six was slightly off the mark. She would have to throw this one away. She grabbed her purse and walked towards the stairs. On her way, she saw something out of the corner of her eye, something floating in the dark. She stopped and stared, then she understood. Two of the younger girls were in the bathroom, and their giggling made Annie's skin crawl.

The light was off but she could see their mouths. Their teeth. One had painted her front teeth and smiled in the mirror. The other had painted a moustache that twirled into spirals on her cheeks. Their nails glowed, too, as they touched their lips and looked at themselves, laughing.

***

Outside was unforgivingly bright, and Annie kept her eyes tight as she walked, only looking up when she came to an intersection. She traced back the way from the day before, and when she came on the block of white row-houses, she became nervous. She saw Vikki's, the fifth one in, and she stared at it.

Once, when she was a teenager, she was watching her baby brother and he fell out of his high chair. It was very quiet for a moment and instead of rushing to him, her first reaction was to step backwards. She wanted to run from him, and the feeling was instinctual, a sudden reflex that took over her entire body. Then he started screaming and she knew she had to move. She liked to think that she waited in the silence because she didn't think he was hurt, but that wasn't it. She knew what it was and she was afraid of it now, but she started moving, anyway.

When she got to the dullest house on the block, she lightly knocked on the door. Someone moved around inside, quickly, then they opened the door. For a moment, Annie was relieved. Vikki seemed just fine. She looked healthier than the day before, to be sure. But then, it wasn't Vikki. Of course, it wasn't. Her hair was more auburn. Brilliantly auburn, and her eyes, while they were blue and shaped like almonds, were brighter and more animated. They looked around intentionally, their lids reacting appropriately.

"I'm sorry," Annie said.

The woman smiled and leaned against the door frame. She reached out as Annie started down the stairs.

"It's alright," she said. "Are you here for Vikki?"

Annie was on the third step of the little cement porch with her hand on the wrought iron railing.

"Is she home?" Annie asked.

Then the woman did a strange thing. It was almost as if she wilted. She looked down at the ground and then back at Annie.

"No, I'm afraid not. She's in the hospital."

Annie didn't answer right away. She thought the woman meant to say something else.

"What for?"

"Would you want to come in? I've cleaned up a little bit since I got here. I've been looking for some of her things, you know, toiletries and what not that I could bring her. It's all been hard to find." The woman walked inside, leaving the door open behind her, and Annie followed.

It looked different with the lights on. Worse. Every surface, including the couch and the chair, had the kind of clutter that collects after too much time and abandon. It reminded Annie of how Frank's apartment looked the first time he invited her upstairs.

"I'm sorry, what's your name? I didn't ask before."

"Annie. I work with Vikki at the factory."

"Nice to meet you, Annie. I'm Viviane, Vikki's older sister."

She picked up magazines and books that had seemed to spread themselves out, and piled them so they could sit. Annie couldn't believe that she was older than Vikki, but then, she wasn't entirely sure how old Vikki was. She couldn't have been too far apart from herself in age.

"Do you know where I might find her pajamas? In case she wants them?"

Annie shook her head.

"Why is she in the hospital? Did she swallow one?"

Viviane's head tilted and her darkly drawn-on brows dropped. Annie put her fingers to her lips and started to pull the bottom one down a bit.

"I'm sorry?" Viviane asked.

"A tooth, I mean."

"Oh," Viviane said. "No. It's a bit more serious than that, I'm afraid. Well, she went to the dentist this morning because of her teeth, and a terrible pain in her jaw. During the . . ." she shifted in her seat and stared at her hands, picking at the skin around her thumb nail. "During the examination, something happened with her jaw bone."

"What bone?"

"The dentist, he was very beside himself when he called me. He sounded so—so frightened. Very upset. He promised he wasn't squeezing, or doing anything too hard, he said he's always very gentle with his female patients. It fell apart, like chalk, he said. Such a strange thing to say about it, but he kept repeating that it felt like chalk snapping in his hand."

"But—" Annie whispered.

Viviane looked up at her and smiled a little.

"The doctors don't know for certain, but they think it's some kind of cancer in her bones. They have her at the hospital now, and fixed it so she can sleep. It's all she really wants to do, anyhow. You said you work with her?"

"Yes."

"Well, I don't think she'll be coming back, but please do tell the girls there where she is. I'm sure she'd love the company. Maybe give it a week or so, so she can get used to talking differently. The doctor said that will be difficult at first, because she won't be able to use parts of her jaw and teeth to press her tongue against. I never thought about that until he said it."

"Sure," Annie said.

Viviane kept the smile on her face while Annie sat on the couch, confused.

"I should get back to the hospital, though. I'll tell her you stopped by."

"Oh." Annie got up so fast that the corners of her vision started to grow shadows. "Please do, thank you. Let me know if she needs anything, or if there's anything I can do." This all came out slower because Annie was trying to say it without pressing her tongue against her bottom row of teeth.

Viviane seemed not to notice as she smiled and quickly nodded. She stayed seated on the couch, as Annie got up and buttoned her coat. Annie could see a tiny drop of blood coming from her thumb's nailbed. She walked toward the door, wanting to get away as fast as she could without being obvious about it. She accidentally bumped her hip against an end table, and she made an unintentionally loud noise at the sharp pain that shot up from it. It didn't matter, though. Viviane wasn't paying attention.

***

Frank had a beer in his hand and an empty one at his feet. Annie's stomach tightened and she marched past him down the hallway into their bedroom. She took off her coat and dropped it on the floor. She felt dirty, like she somehow tracked the grime from Vikki's house back with her and it was spreading on her skin. She pictured tiny bugs in her hair and under her clothes, and she thought she could feel them crawling with their tiny legs and their tiny mouths making tiny holes in which to burrow. She undressed quickly, popping a stitch at her waist as she yanked the dress over her head. She stepped into the shower and turned it as hot as it would go, standing underneath the water until her hands turned viciously red and steam had filled the room.

"Annie, can I talk to you?"

Annie screamed. She hadn't heard Frank come in. She turned the water off and stood behind the curtain holding her arms up against her with her hands in fists underneath her chin. Frank pulled the curtain over and his face went dark.

"Jesus, Annie. What happened to your hip?"

She looked down and saw the spot she had hit before. A large, dark red mark had already formed. It was so dark it looked brown.

"I ran into a table. I didn't even notice it."

He knelt down on the tile floor, grabbing the back of her thighs to bring her closer to him.

"It looks like it hurt you," he said, brushing his thumb over it.

He looked up at her and she put her hands on the top of his head. He bowed towards her again, pressing against her with his mouth. She stroked his hair, pulling strands between her fingers as he put his lips on it. He leaned back and grabbed her hand, kissing it before he stood up, and pulled her with him into the bedroom. As she walked behind him, she saw the way his fingers were knotted and greasy with oil, and how she liked the way it looked against her beet red skin. He turned out the light as she was staring at their hands, but she could still see them. She could still see hers. Her eyes needed no adjusting. There, faintly in the dark, she could still see the way her hand held his. She could see the way her knuckles bent and her fingers gripped against him. An iridescent light came out from her, illuminating her nails and the bones that raked the back of her hand. She could see herself. She was glowing from the inside, now.

The Radium Girls from Ottawa, IL found gainful employment with the Illinois Radium Dial Company in the 20s, their small female fingers better able to paint the glow-in-the-dark radium paint. Soon, the workers became ill and then they started dying. They wanted justice. They formed a group that was known as The Society of the Living Dead and fought hard for acknowledgment and any compensation they could leave to their families. The women in Illinois were the only radium workers in the US to gain any legal compensation.

"And it hurts to smile, but I still smile."
–Grace Fryer, a Radium Girl

Chapter Fourteen

The Hive Broke on a Sunday

Franklin Township, NJ. 1922

For two days, two people laid dead underneath a crabapple tree in the Franklin township of New Jersey. A man and a woman lay in the sun, on the ground with the fallen crabapples that became rotten and eaten by bees that were still crawling all over them. She hated bees but there was nothing she could do about it. They smelled bad, the both of them. She was waiting for someone to come and find them, someone to stumble upon the scene and hurt their lungs with screaming.

While her hand had been on his thigh for two nights and his arm stretched underneath her torn neck, she wondered if the Sunday paper would include a picture of them, or would they have to wait until Monday. She tried to imagine the date, but she wasn't sure what day it was. May something, 1922, that's all she could think of. Her neck, once long and slender, had been truncated, and her vocal cords were gone. There was no way she could sing on Sundays now.

E's Panama hat was covering up his face, like he was sleeping and didn't want the sun in his eyes. She had gotten that hat for E when she was down in Florida with her husband. Her husband had a reputation at being good at cleaning things up and nothing else. She told him she was out buying him a gift, he never asked when he'd get it, which was fine because he never did.

"They call it a panama hat because you can roll it up and stuff it in one of those cigar tubes."

"That's very kind, but you know I don't smoke," E said.

"That doesn't mean you can't put it on, you can roll it up and stick it in your pocket when you're not wearing it. Look at that," *she pulled the hat down on his head, rubbing it against his bald spots, making sure it was on tight. "It suits you."*

"Whatever you say, darling."

There was a sound behind them, someone who was most certainly walking, had come to a stop.

"Hey, hold it," A girl said. Just a teenager.

"What, baby? I see some bushes over there, we can sit behind those," the man said. He was a bit older, just a little too much.

"Look over there, do you see those people lying down?"

"I don't see no one, come on, you're stalling." The man bundled up the sides of her dress in his fists, pulling her closer to him while he stuck his nose in her hair.

"Quit. Look, by the tree. You see them? The black-haired woman and the man in the white suit. Looks like they're sleeping."

We aren't sleeping, please, look at us, we're not breathing.

"Then let's let them alone and go somewhere else."

"Jimmy, they look strange."

"So, what?"

The two moved a little closer to the other two on the ground.

"Come on, Pearl, let's get out of here, do you smell that?"

That's us, you dumb fool.

They ran, like she thought they would. Jimmy was awkward about it, taking wide crab steps around the back of Pearl who wasn't moving fast enough for him. He was straining himself not to be the first one out of there. Trying hard to balance being a gentleman and a coward.

***

She walked up the aisle and saw him at the podium, whispering to himself and making sweeping gestures with his hands. She could tell that Sunday would be a day where the sheep got scolded for their sins.

"E, take me to the basement, I have to get home soon and finish up a dress for Charlotte."

"I'm almost finished writing."

"But you're not writing."

E tapped the shiny top of his head with his finger. "Just a moment."

She took a seat in the second row pew and put her hands between her thighs. No matter how warm it was, she felt cold in an empty church. The draft was always on the back of her neck. She watched

*more of his gestures and he looked out in her direction, but he
didn't see her.*

***

Officers Edward Ervin and John Todd walked onto the grass
from the road like people who weren't looking to help anyone.

"The girl said they were lying right underneath a crabapple
tree, do you see one around?" Said Ervin.

"Is that one? Over there?" Todd asked. Todd had more en-
thusiasm, like he had two more cups of coffee than Ervin before
they left the station.

"Let's take a look." Ervin said. Even his words were lazy.

They walked up to the pair on the ground and Ervin leaned
in while Todd stayed away with his hand up to his mouth and
his fingers pinching his nose. Ervin stared long and hard at her
while Todd kept his eyes on the crabapples.

"Does she look familiar to you?"

"No, sir, I haven't seen her."

"You're still not seeing her, come over here, and lift the man's
hat, let's take a look at his face."

Officer Todd lifted E's hat off his face and more flies flew
away. His glasses weren't broken, which was miraculous con-
sidering he had been shot in the head.

"Don't know him either."

"Check his wallet."

Todd started opening up E's pockets, pinching his suit coat and holding it out between his fingers like he was afraid he was going to catch his death. More flies came at him.

This isn't right, this isn't how this should be done. They're doing it all wrong.

"Edward Wheeler Hall, says he's from New Brunswick."

"That means it's ours."

"I don't know, we'll have to call up Franklin and Middlesex, we're standing on the borders.

***

"How are you feeling, song bird? Can you sing for us?"

"Edward, don't even joke about that, she's just out of surgery. She'll do it just to make you happy and you know it." E's wife gestured toward E, but didn't actually touch him.

"I'm sorry dear, I'm sure she knows that I'm only teasing her, isn't that right?" E asked.

"Just worry about getting your rest so you can get home as fast as you can to that husband and those darlings. I'm sure they miss you." Mrs. Hall said while she leaned forward in her chair, showing her all of the teeth in her mouth.

She touched her throat a little, just enough to let Mrs. Hall know that she was thirsty or in pain, whatever made her go away.

"Do you want some water? I'll run and grab the nurse."

Mrs. Hall padded the bottom of her gray haired bun and straightened her skirt before walking out of the room. "Edward, you leave her alone."

E kept looking at her while his wife left them. He snaked his hand underneath the blanket so just the tips of his fingers were touching her right knee. He looked at her and she closed her eyes and swallowed. He looked down at the lump in the blanket and brought the other hand out of his pocket. She moved her knee, just a little, she wasn't even sure he knew that anything had happened until she saw him staring at her with his eyelids halfway down.

"I would." The words scratched out of her throat.

"What did you say?" E leaned closer to her, putting his hand flush on her knee, grabbing it to brace himself.

***

With the Franklin and Middlesex police departments came a few neighbors who had seen the cars crowding De Russey's lane. Half a dozen of them stood around the tree, hugging their arms to their chests and stretching their necks over each other. A low hum had started. Lots of "have you heard anything?" and "who are they?" A few people asked, "how'd they die," or, "how'd they get it?" and a funny man with real sharp elbows said, "what's got them down?"

"I heard they found a bunch of love letters around the bodies, could be they were fooling around behind someone's back," said a man with his pant legs rolled up.

"I haven't heard of many faithfully married people ending up in the dirt like this unless the preacher put them in it," another man said.

"I was talking to a reporter from the Daily and he said it was Reverend Hall from St. John's, near the river in New Brunswick."

"They arrested somebody already?"

"No, he said the dead man was the reverend, didn't say anything about who did it. Said the reverend was lying there with a woman, her neck is all messed up."

"Who's she?"

Please, please say it.

"Didn't know."

People kept rolling up in their cars, all shiny, like they had gotten them washed for the occasion. Children in church dresses and little suits spilled out of them, running towards the crowd. Most of them stayed within the circle of people, snaking around. Others stood just outside the group, kicking around rotted out crabapples and running from the bees they made angry.

"Mama, can I eat this?"

"Stop picking things up off the ground, look at all this mud on your Sunday dress, drop that, right now."

The little blonde girl dropped the spotted crabapple and watched it roll away from her, down the small hill towards the man with his camera as he flashed lights at the bodies on the ground. She put her hand in front of her face and stretched out her fingers while she licked her palm. Her mother batted her hand away "Mary, stop it, that's disgusting."

"It tastes sour, I like sour things."

"I'm going to wash your mouth out with soap when we get home."

The girl clapped both hands together over her mouth and furiously shook her whole body from side to side.

Slowly, other things were getting picked up or scratched off and put in pockets. Porkpie men were pulling out their little knives and sticking them into the tree, either taking off the bark or leaving a few letters.

***

"What do you think about the plan?" she said.

"What plan?" E said.

"God's plan. Do you think he has one for us?"

"A preacher wouldn't be worth his salt if he didn't believe in a divine plan. All of God's children have something in store for them, something that is going to touch the lives of all the rest. Like strand of a spider web. One strand has no idea about the other strand across the web, but they are both relying on each other for structure."

"Structure, that's the plan then?"

"Structure, order, everyone works together. Like a machine, like a car. You see, you can have a good engine, but a good engine without the body just sits in the dirt. You need all the parts. The engine doesn't know its purpose until it's done being made and they put it into the perfect shaped hole. Then the whole picture comes to life."

"The engine never knows anything at all."

"It's just a metaphor."

"It doesn't work for me."

"What do you think?"

"I don't know, this seems out of line," she said.

He moved his hand from her breast and rolled her so she was facing him. He touched her neck and then pulled on her ear while he smiled at her.

"Do you feel like we're sinning?" E asked.

"This is sinning."

"Do you feel wrong inside?"

"It doesn't matter."

"But it does, it matters the most. I'm a man of faith and I believe that this means more than the shame you're bringing to it. It's not necessary, we would be lying to God if we weren't together. You don't feel that?"

"I feel it," she said.

"What we do together, it's like a prayer. Do you remember what Jesus said? I think about that verse all the time, when Jesus says, 'wherever two or more are gathered in my name, that's where I am,' I feel Jesus when we're together. The Holy Light."

As he said the last word, he put his hand in between her legs and hooked up into her while she exhaled out, "Oh, Christ."

***

"My sister-in-law goes to St. John's, she said everyone knew he was messing around with a choir girl," said a woman with her arms crossed over her breasts. She was clutching at them like she was cold.

"Has anyone told his wife? Has she been here today?"

"I don't think so, I heard she's a few years older than him, and there weren't any kids."

"Who's the girl?"

"Don't know."

What good are you? Spreading gossip that isn't even yours, helping nobody in the process.

They propped her up on the rollaway stretcher, a rusty thing that seemed like it would break with her small body on top of it. A small clearing was made around the tree. Her head rolled to the right and her eyes were open.

She saw the horrible thing that she didn't want to know about. The people of the God-fearing, church-going town had come out for them. The crowd had grown to a size that looked like half the world. They had swarmed them and spoke so fast, they sounded just like the bees. The crabapple tree, their temporary grave marker, had been stripped of all its bark. It looked like an exposed muscle that people scratched their names into. The people had descended like locusts and stole its skin for a souvenir. She prayed someone would close her eyes.

> *The married pastor and the choir girl found dead, together, underneath a crabapple tree in 1922 caused the good people of New Brunswick to come witness in their Sunday best a social spectacle. People were so enraptured with the scene that they, like killers, took souvenirs, completely stripping the tree from they lay underneath of all its bark. The Halls-Mills murders have never been solved.*

One grows slightly dizzy, but hangs stubbornly to the notion that the modern murder trial, of which the Hall-Mills case is a singularly fine example, is something less than perfect as a means of establishing the guilt of accused men and women. But as a spectacle, an ironic spectacle, full of juicy chuckles, ah!
–The New Yorker

Chapter Fifteen

Playing House

Lincoln, NE. 1958

L et's play pretend. I'll get the good china set out, and you run to the store and grab some soda.

"Beer?" you ask.

But I've only ever had sips before from the half-empty bottles my folks leave out around the house. It never tasted so good. It was always warm and flat and sour.

"It's better when it's cold. I'll show you. We'll keep it on ice."

But the icebox is outside, I don't think I want to go outside, yet.

"I'll go, then."

That's nice.

I pull out the china from the built-in cabinet in the dining room. The doors stick because we never ever opened these. Mama got them from her first wedding with Daddy—from Daddy's mama. Then Mama kicked Daddy out. She changed the locks on the doors and he didn't try very hard to get past that inconvenience. She never used them, but she didn't want to sell them.

They are covered in dust, now. They are just covered in dust so thick that when I drag my finger in the shape of a heart on a dinner plate, it cakes instead of gathers. A dark-gray thick smudge instead of seeing white bone underneath. Mama should have cleaned these from time to time.

I set the table for two. Two dinner plates, two little plates, and then the cheap nickel forks and knives that look like a play set my baby sister uses. But when I think about that I feel funny, so I don't think about it, and I don't touch them anymore. They are all cold and stiff.

"What are we gonna eat?" you ask, in a kind of way that doesn't remind me of my stepdaddy and I smile a little. You're real good at making me smile. I won't forget that.

I tell you to check the fridge. Maybe there is something in there. I hope there is because I don't want to tell you. I don't want to spoil anything, but I ain't much of a cook. My Mama kept us out of the kitchen to keep herself sane, she'd always tell us. She'd always yell it. She was always too loud.

"Meatloaf? Looks bad though."

You show it to me. Your black leather jacket bunches around your shoulders as you cradle this small glass pan in your dirty hands. I peek. With my own fingers—my pink painted nails that now are all chipped and broken, I touch it. The ketchup hardened into an ugly crusted zig-zag over the top. There is one slice taken out. Unless Mama split that up and meant for the baby to have one half for dinner now and one half for dinner tomorrow. But I don't want to think about that. I don't mean to think about what the baby's mouth looks like now.

"You see the mold?" you ask.

I do. Some blue and white fuzz sprouting off the ground beef. You scrunch up your face and it looks strange. You look ugly, and my stomach turns a little. I tell you to just cut that part off and heat it up in the oven.

"Really? That's alright?"

Why wouldn't it be?

"I won't get sick?"

No, I say. But I think I don't know what gets you sick.

"How long should I put it in?"

I don't know so I say an hour. I tell you to twist the egg timer all the way around.

"Alright," you say, and you are so unsure that it makes me feel sorry for you—in a bad way. My cheeks get hot. I think we shouldn't have done this. But we didn't do nothing.

You turn around and disappear into the kitchen. We haven't cleaned the kitchen good enough, I suspect, so I don't follow you in there. I picture it all hard and crusted over the linoleum floor or the yellow counters. I don't know where it all got, I make myself think. I make myself think I might not even know it's there.

I walk back into the dining room. It looks dirty because the curtains are all closed and the little light getting in makes everything kind of brown. Dirty and dark. The table has two big plates, two small plates, two knives, and two forks. But I'm wrong. I can't see so good in the dark. There are five big plates, five small plates, five knives, and five forks. And a shotgun. The baby is playing with it, I think. She's picking it up and dropping it, making a bad sound, like one of those pop-up boxes that's meant to scare you. Mama is gripping her butter knife—but I think it's a butcher knife. She knocks it against the table, making another bad sound. They're all so loud—except my stepdaddy. He's quiet. He's got something he's trying to get out of his throat. You come into the dining room like a dog following me.

"What do you want to do while we wait?" you ask.

I think you mean to try something with me. Something physical. I see that your face has a smile on it that I've seen before. A look you get when you're about to hit someone for no reason. I like that look. I take your hand, and before I lead you upstairs, I look, again, at the table. They're all still there, but you don't see them. They're all still making noise, but you don't hear them. Mama, in particular, looks real mad. She hates you.

The stairs creak and the baby's room is right at the top. The door is open. I ask you to close it, even though she's not in there. Maybe she is—maybe I don't know. I take you past Mama's room and through the side of my eye I can see the covers piled up in the middle of the bed, I can almost think she's taking a nap. She's just waiting for Betty Jean to wake up. And scream and scream because mama moves too slow like she can't hear it and that child has a set of lungs on it that reach down and wring your spine with crazy sound. But that's alright. She's quiet now, and you and I can be secret.

We get to my room. It's small. All the things in it look like someone else's now. I don't know why. I get sad, real sad all of a sudden, because I guess I know we can't stay here very long. Even I know people won't think we all have the flu forever.

Mama's work is gonna call. School is gonna call. They'll send the truancy officer down and we'd be dumber than rocks to be answering the door. I sniffle, because I want you to know I'm sad.

"Darling," you say, just like I planned on you saying, but now it doesn't sound the same.

"You know I'll take care of everything, right? You know I will," you say. And maybe you will. Maybe we can leave and get ourselves a nice little house away from all the pigs and chickens and shit where we put them—no no no no no, where you put them. Where I don't know. Mama is sleeping. Betty is sleeping. My stepdaddy is working or maybe he's even being real quiet out in the shed because he's laying face down on that thin wood board that shouldn't even be able to hold his fat ass, as all the chickens hop around his quiet self. From my room, I can hear them chickens. They're upset that they've been disturbed.

"Come sit next to me." You're on my bed now. You pat my yellow daisy quilt with your dirty hand. I come over. I sit down and your weight in the bed makes me lean towards you when I'm not sure that's what I want to do. But you don't do nothing, really. You put your hand on my back and start rubbing it. But then I kiss you so we can get this done.

Later, we walk back down the hall to the stairs, passing my still-sleeping mama and my still-sleeping sister. What time is it? How long have they been asleep? It's a little darker in the house. You're a little disappointed. I'm a little glad it's over. I walk in front of you so I don't have to contend with the way your shoulders slouch. The bottom of the stairs looks completely black. Like maybe there isn't even a floor there anymore. But, even if I'm scared of the dark, I'll keep walking, because I smell something burning.

"What is that?" you ask.

It's the meatloaf, dummy. I run into the kitchen. I turn on the light but I shouldn't have. I should have thought. I should have fumbled in the dark and burned my own hands instead. But I'm just as dumb as you because I am so surprised when the light comes on and shows everything we missed. I can't shut my eyes, but I want to. You charge ahead and open up the stove and smoke floats out across the room, and I still see everything. There are bits of mama's hair on the walls like spaghetti noodles.

"It's all black," you say, but her hair is red.

Scrape it off. It ain't burned all the way through, there's something in the middle there that's good. There's got to be. Before you can say anything, I get out of there. I go back to the dining room. They're all still there. They're all still waiting. Mama has her knife ready. Betty has the butt of the shotgun in her mouth, working her gums around it because she's teething. You come in and you still don't see them. You put the meatloaf in the middle of the table. Mama bangs her butcher knife when your hand gets close to her. She wants to stick you with it so bad, but she can't because you were stronger. Stepdaddy wants to scream and holler at you, but he can't because you gave him such a surprise. And Betty Jean is only looking at me but she don't know no better, because I don't know a thing.

Caril Ann Fugate started dating Charles Starkweather when she was 13 years old and he was 18. He was a high school dropout and she was an innocent little kid, or was she? By the time she was 14, her entire family was murdered and after a week hiding out in her family home with the bodies decomposing around them, she fled with Starkweather on a cross-country rampage ending with seven more dead. Her level of complicity has always been in question. Their story inspired "Natural Born Killers" and Bruce Springsteen's "Nebraska". Charles Starkweather was put to death in 1959 and Caril Ann Fugate was paroled in 1976. She has been free ever since, though her appeals for a pardon have been denied.

"She wishes she could wash everything away."
–Tom Clair, Caril Ann Fugate's stepson

Chapter Sixteen

Wonderland

Nancy knew that the river had always been dirty. She didn't know what was underneath. She didn't know about the junked rides from the old amusement park. How the rails of the Milwaukee Motorway twisted through the mud, and would occasionally disappear underneath the layer of shifting sediment. How the Ferris Wheel laid out broken on its side, and how the river bottom grew up around it, making six muck caves out of the cars where things could hide. She didn't know about the Electrical Tower, fallen over and studded with shattered light bulbs, cutting through the bend of the river like a broken bone.

As Nancy watched a police officer zip into a black, rubber wetsuit she couldn't help but feel filthy and polluted. She had never really been friends with the Kings, but she wondered if they thought the same. She had the occasional glass of wine on their back porch, and they invited her for dinner, but she often denied them. Nancy wasn't the only person down by the river, but she tried to stick close to the trail in case she needed to hop on and start walking. She wasn't as brazen as the people who were right up on the yellow tape, she thought. But that wasn't true. She had seen the police walking quickly down the trail behind her house, and she followed them, as if it were any of her business.

It was close, which surprised her, even though she knew she shouldn't be surprised. If it really was Jessica, she wouldn't have gone far—that's what the Kings' had said at the press conference where Melissa smiled so much. That had been noticed. A few people there had come from the beer garden holding half-filled liters. They were the generally curious, naturally responding to some activity near them. The way she waited by the trail was pretend. If anyone asked her what was going on, she would lie and say, "I don't know, I was just walking by." Nancy imagined Jessica's red hair, and how it would float under water, away from her, reaching out like strands of pale, fiberglass lights being dimmed by the dark.

The river was good at hiding things.

***

The morning that Jessica had gone missing, Melissa showed up at her door. Nancy had gone out the night before and a man she couldn't quite remember meeting was sleeping in her bed. He had black hair all over his back and she was afraid it might stain her sheets. She wasn't thinking clearly. She prepared herself to be yelled at. Their houses were unfortunately close, with the Kings' kitchen window lining up perfectly with Nancy's bedroom window. Had they been too loud? What things did she scream when the man fucked her? She thought of Linda Blair in *The Exorcist*, and she squinted her eyes even though the sun didn't hit her face. But then Melissa smiled.

"I'm sorry," Melissa said. "I'm sorry to bother you, but we can't find her."

"Who?"

"Jessica, she's not inside. You haven't seen her? Or maybe she stopped by?"

The suggestion was farfetched, Nancy only ever waved at her when Jessica screamed, "Hi," from the front lawn. Jessica seemed frustrated when she did it. Indignant attention seeking–Nancy could relate. But, this had only happened when Nancy and Jessica were awake and moving in the world at the same time, so once or twice. They had never formally met. Suddenly, Nancy heard a man scream somewhere close, and she thought it might be the strange man in her bedroom, but it was Joe, calling out Jessica's full name. Her middle name was Joy and it was strange hearing that word shouted in desperation.

"Oh," Nancy said. "No, I haven't seen her. I've been asleep."

"She was in her room, and I took a shower. I thought Joe was up, but he fell asleep on the couch. He's been sick."

"Right."

"Anyway, she was gone when I came back in."

The zipper on Nancy's sweatshirt hit her bare skin and the cold stunned her.

"Here, let me get a coat on and I'll come help you look. I'm sure she just went to a friend's house." Could a 4-year-old know about running away? Did they remember how to get places?

"Thank you so much," Melissa said. "We'll be in back of the house, or near it, if you want to walk up and down the block and knock on a few doors, that would be great." Nancy didn't want to do that.

She went back into the house and to her kitchen window that overlooked the trail. She stared at the dark pavement, then into the trees and bushes, until she forced herself to go into her bedroom. She opened the door slowly, but he was already sitting up and rubbing his neck as he faced her closet. He still had his clothes off, and she couldn't stop staring at his back.

"Hi," she said.

"Oh, hey," he said, turning to look at her. She wished he wouldn't.

"So, my neighbors can't find their kid."

"Huh."

"I was going to help them look for a bit," she said.

"Let me just get some clothes on and I'll go with you."

"No, you don't have to."

"It's fine, can't hurt to have more people out there. What's her name?"

Nancy thought for a moment, but there was no good way she could tell him to go home, that their transgression had ended. They went out together, one going north and the other south.

"Skip the pink house," she told him, and he nodded, scanning the rest of the houses as if he was counting them. She wondered what he did for work.

She finished before him. At first, she believed this was a good thing—efficient. But while she waited on her cement steps, getting more uncomfortable as her jeans let in the cold from the ground, she felt nervous. Did her strange man find her? Did he meet up with Melissa or Joe and rejoin them already? Had she missed it? Finally, she saw him, walking back with his hands stuffed into the front pocket of his hoodie. He looked defeated.

"Nothing," he said.

Before he left he asked her to let him know what happened. If they found Jessica, he said. Her name came out of his mouth without any hesitation, which put Nancy off. He was just a stranger, after all.

The police came later, around dusk. One parked in the King's driveway, and the other drove around the neighborhood, slowly. They both had their lights on but left their sirens off, and it looked very strange, as if they had been muted. One of the officers showed up at her door, asking again if she had seen Jessica. Nancy told them no, but that she looked for a while that morning.

"And did anything come from that?"

She was embarrassed. "No," she said.

"Well, if you see her, or think of anything, give us a call," he said. He handed her a card and walked to the next house, where a couple she had met earlier, and still couldn't name, waited at the door.

The neighbors gathered in front of the Kings' house, that night. They had flashlights that kept sweeping into Nancy's house. She watched as they went to the trail and then back into the woods and brush, their lights streaming and blinking in and out. Nancy didn't think she had a flashlight.

***

She showed up to the first official daytime search party. They met in the middle of the street, this way, Melissa said, if people wanted to get through they would have to ask what was going on. As if they didn't know already. Jessica's picture was somehow already everywhere, printed with the concrete details of her person, everything she could have possibly been; *Age 4, Strawberry Blonde Hair, Blue Eyes, 40 Inches Tall, 39 Pounds. Last seen in her room.* They ran her face on the news, with Melissa still smiling and talking beside it. "She loves animals," she had said.

"Okay, everyone," Melissa shouted to the crowd. Nancy didn't know how many people were there, she was never very good at guessing how many gumballs were in the jar, but the crowd was large. "These are the places that Jessica knows."

She handed out maps with playgrounds and the grocery store highlighted in fluorescent pink. Her handwriting was perfect, as if she were replying to a wedding invitation instead of writing down the spots her missing daughter had frequented. *Jessica liked to watch the dogs here*, with a beautiful X crossing over the dog park. It took a moment before she realized that Melissa was giving directions. She talked too fast, and then trailed off. As Nancy watched her, she noticed that one of Melissa's eyes kept drifting. When Melissa finished, she clapped her hands together and Nancy expected her to jump in the air.

"Let's go everyone, let's find our girl!" But Jessica wasn't their girl.

***

The search party numbers rapidly declined. The news conference had changed things. She woke up to the noises that morning, the loud murmuring outside of her small house. Nancy half opened her eyes, squinting as her contacts squeezed them tightly. Her TV was on but the volume was low, too low to be the source of the sound. Then she saw the side of her house on the screen and instinctively put a hand over her face.

She went to her front window and spread the blinds with her fingers. A massive crowd spilled over onto her lawn from the Kings' front porch, where Melissa was holding a piece of paper and a cupcake, and Joe stood behind her, looking down. Nancy ran back to her room and watched.

"Hey, everyone! Thank you so much for coming today because it's a very special day, today, wow, I'm saying that word a lot." Melissa laughed. "But, today is Jessica's fifth birthday and we just wanted to let everyone know that we haven't forgotten and we want to celebrate with you all."

She started singing and held the cupcake out in front of her. She interrupted herself after the first "happy birthday to you," and said, "come on, help me out." That's when Nancy could hear them from her bedroom, a slow and awkward song that sounded more like people talking at once than singing. Joe kept his mouth closed but he started swaying back and forth a little. There was a two second delay and at the end she heard a few them clap before she saw Melissa blow out the candle.

"Take a bite," she said, handing it to Joe. He waved it away without even glancing at it.

She laughed, then said, "Does anyone else want it?"

Nobody said a word, and most of them turned their heads away.

"Well, can't let it go to waste," she said. She took a big bite, without restraint. The frosting stained her teeth instantly.

***

The first snow came just before Christmas and the flyer taped to the cement light pole outside Nancy's work was slipping. Jessica's face had started to warp. The top of her head was protected under the layers of scotch tape, and you could see the part in her hair, but her cheeks and nose had melted. You could still see the row of baby teeth in-between her lips. Nancy thought about taking it down and replacing it later, but the thought of touching it made her wipe her hand down her coat.

The restaurant was small, and the smell of garlic hit her first thing as she walked in the door. She hated it now. There were only a handful of people dining, which was as many as there ever were. Inside the glass menu case at the front was another flyer, this one well preserved and hanging perfectly straight. On it, you could see that the sundress she was wearing had red and yellow balloons on it, floating up towards her neck.

Nancy took a basket of bread over to a two-top and set it down. While she arranged the oil and vinegar, and placed the small plates in front of two faceless people, she half listened to their conversation about how much homework their kids had. In the beginning, any mention of children would dredge up Jessica's name. "Those poor parents," and "I can't imagine."

The phrases that flow out of people's mouths when they're automatically responding to something while thinking about something else. You can imagine, of course you can, Nancy would think. It's not difficult.

Once, a woman had told the other woman she was with that she would never have bought a house so close to the river. It's like living on a busy street, she said.

"I live next to the river, and it's fine. Beautiful," Nancy said.

The woman was taken aback, and leaned away from her.

"Do you have kids?" The woman asked.

"Sure," Nancy said. They didn't leave a tip.

By mid-December, a month after Jessica disappeared, the conversations changed, and the phrases were altered. "But, those parents," and "can you imagine?" They didn't whisper this like they had before. They didn't treat their words carefully.

When she got home that night, she pulled into her driveway and her lights caught something in the distance. Melissa was walking away from her house. Nancy could only see the pale skin of her back as she disappeared down the small hill. It was like seeing a ghost. Nancy got out of her car and ran over to the edge of her backyard, but she couldn't see Melissa. She shouted her name, once, but the sound of it reminded her of Joe's "Joy," and she clapped a hand over her mouth. She stood as the snow fell over the tops of her shoes, hitting her socks and skin.

***

She had forgotten how she met the strange man but he was apparently a bartender working a few blocks away from her house, and that made sense—Nancy didn't like to go too far. Nancy hadn't gone out in a while, the winter forced her inside like a mouse. He was playing bar dice when she walked in and he slammed the shaker down hard enough that the sound bounced off the door that had closed behind her. He saw her before she could turn around, and he smiled. She gave him a small wave and walked up to the bar.

"Hey, there," he said, coming over to her.

"Hi," she said. "How are you?"

"Good, what can I get you?"

"A PBR is fine, thanks."

"Tallboy?"

"Sure."

He turned and bent over to get in the fridge. His shirt lifted up showing the small of his back and Nancy closed her eyes.

"Your friend's playing pool," he said.

"Sorry?"

"Your neighbor, you know . . ." He stared at her, not quite knowing how to describe her. Then she saw her.

Melissa smiled and threw her head back as she touched the arm of the man at the pool table with her. He was barely a man, he looked young. The two of them together made it seem like Melissa was a young mother with her adult son.

"I called you a few times." He smiled.

"I got a new phone," she said. Nancy never answered numbers she didn't know, but she wouldn't have answered if she did.

Nancy dug her nails under the tab, and kept watching her neighbor. Finally, Melissa saw her, and she waved before running over. She smelled like hard alcohol and perfume.

"Nancy!" she said. "How are you? I haven't seen you."

"Melissa, are you okay?"

"Actually, I'm thirsty. Let's have my friend get us some drinks." She waved him over, furiously.

"Nancy, this is my friend Zak, he's an art student, like I was. Look at his hands!" She grabbed them and pushed them into Nancy's face. They were stained with blue paint in the nail beds and creases in-between his fingers. His hair was long and brown, with an unkempt beard and muddy eyes.

"I was thinking we could head back, soon." He leaned over Melissa saying it into the top of her hair.

"He's going to show me something he's working on. Do you want to come?"

"Melissa, do you think that's a good idea? I mean, wouldn't Joe worry about where you are?"

"It won't take too long."

"Why don't you stay for a while?"

"The building's going to close soon," Zak said.

"I think we're going to go now. But it was good seeing you." Melissa said the last part as if she was leaving a party at someone's house because she was tired.

"No, wait." But before Nancy could get off her stool, Melissa was already at the door. When she got outside, she saw Melissa running, a block down, holding her shoes in her hands and laughing as her breath steamed out of her mouth.

Nancy went home with the strange man whose name was Rob. This time things were clearer, though she was good and drunk. There were no animal noises, no demonic screams, and they both kept their shirts on. Rob left before she woke up.

***

When Spring came, everyone waited. If someone went in while it was cold, the river held onto the body until the temperature rose, the gasses expanding causing it to become buoyant and float up to the top like turned over dead fish. Nancy looked through her blinds when she woke up and went to sleep, as if she were checking an alarm. But nothing changed. After the grass had grown to an embarrassing height, Nancy rolled out her lawnmower but couldn't get it started.

"It's out of gas," Joe said. He stood behind her on his side of the dip between their lawns.

"Right," she said. "Shit."

"I have some in mine, I'll bring it over and take care of it."

"No, no, don't worry about it. I'll run over to the gas station and fill up the thing."

"I'll be right back."

Joe's arms shook as he cut the yard. He started sweating around the collar of his shirt and in his armpits, even though the lawn was small. Finally, when he finished, he let the bar snap back from his hands, keeping them rested on the handle.

"Thank you," Nancy said from where she sat on the steps. She was apprehensive about going up to him.

He nodded, breathing deeply.

"Melissa's been acting strange," he said, abruptly.

Nancy stared at him. He wasn't looking back, narrowing his eyes at his house.

"I'm sure it's hard," Nancy said.

"She walks around the house at night, she can't sleep. I can't sleep, either, but she's talking to herself. She comes back to bed in the morning and she's not wearing anything, but when I look, I can't find her clothes. I don't know where she's putting them.

"You should see her, sometime. She could use a little, I don't know, distraction. Maybe you could take her out? The house is hard for her. She doesn't like to be around here." He twirled his finger around.

"Okay. Sure," she said.

***

After they brought Jessica up, the police gave an update. They said there was no indication of foul play, and she died from drowning brought on by hypothermia. They didn't say that her muscles tore after twisting in the cold. They said her body had gotten stuck down there, but didn't elaborate. There was no mention of the Ferris Wheel. Nancy fell asleep early that night, but she didn't sleep well as she dreamt of being underwater for too long. When she snapped her eyes open, she felt coiled like wire. Lines of light slashed over her from Nancy's bedroom window that looked into the Kings house. She turned and saw Melissa in their kitchen, sitting at a table with a drawing in her hand. She wasn't looking at the drawing, but out the sliding glass doors into the dark. It was a messy picture, on a piece of tan coloring book paper. A pair of blue and green horses stood side by side. Jessica's name was smeared over the top; she had painted it with her fingers, leaving prints all over. Nancy suddenly wanted to call Rob and tell him that they found her, but she didn't know his number.

The next morning, she woke up and saw Melissa with her head down on the table and her arms spread out in front of her, almost unnaturally long. It scared Nancy, and she hit her window with her palm. Melissa didn't move and so she did it again—in rapid succession like a large bird trying to get into her house, or out of it. Melissa shot up in the chair, her face red on one side with the crease from the table leaf cutting through her cheek. They stared at one another from their own houses, until Melissa got up and walked to the sliding doors. Nancy crawled out of bed and walked to the backdoor. Melissa stood in her yard, looking towards the river.

"I'm sorry I scared you," Melissa said.

"No, it's fine. I just thought . . ."

"I know. I think I scare everybody, all the time."

"I'm sorry," Nancy said, and before she could stop herself she said, "I can't imagine."

"Do you want to take a walk with me?"

Nancy walked with her down the Oakleaf trail, they went slowly and started drifting closer together. Melissa stopped and went left into the woods on a smaller unmarked dirt trail that took them both down to the river. There, a long pile of rocks reached out into the water like a makeshift pier.

"It's like dying but staying alive, even though you're all dead, every part of you," Melissa said.

"I'm sorry," Nancy said again.

"They found her underneath a Ferris Wheel. There's old rides down there from an amusement park that used to be nearby. They just threw them in the river when they closed the park. I wished they'd kept it. It would have been nice to have that kind of thing close."

Nancy thought of wet and rotting rollercoasters, all of the cars sloshing with mud and slop as they jerked along the track.

"We never even took her to the fair. Is that funny? I took her here, to this spot. She named it, but then kept renaming it. I don't know what it was last," Melissa said.

"I'm sure she loved it."

"She must have been so cold. I tried to understand," Melissa said. She picked up a small rock from the water and held it in her hand before she put in her pocket.

"No one's out here. No fishing or kayaking. Seems strange, no?" Melissa asked.

"You're right."

Nancy walked to the last rocks, letting the water creep up on her feet. Maybe people were afraid to go in. To fall or get caught up in something they couldn't see. The park was bigger than anything they thought could be beneath them. The rides could float up, dirty and bloated just the same as Jessica. Underneath the muddy brown surface were long twisting tracks, carousel horses that had once been colorful bared their teeth, and fallen towers covered in shattered lightbulbs rested in wait. Somewhere, too, there was an iron gate that said, "Welcome to Wonderland." Nancy didn't want to know what was down there. She didn't want to see underneath.

In 1992, in Milwaukee, WI, I went missing when I was with my babysitter. I was four. Here are two news clippings From the Milwaukee Journal Sentinel:

1. The girl's baby sitter told the parents that her husband, who is in his mid-30s, dropped her off at the dentist office near Northridge Shopping center and said he was taking the girl to a nearby McDonald's restaurant. The man told his wife he would return about 3:00 p.m. The man never returned and the baby sitter eventually took a bus back to her Wauwatosa home at about 5 p.m. The girl, who turned 4 last week, is a bout 40 inches tall and weighs about 40 pounds. She dark blond, chin-length hair. She was wearing a three-quarter length, bright multicolored jacket with a draw-string around the middle.

2. A 4-year-old girl reported missing Thursday night was returned to her parents' home early Friday morning, police reported. The girl, whose parents reported her missing Thursday evening, was returned around 2 a.m. Friday, Police said. Police refused to say who returned the girl or where she had been during the hours she was missing. Police did say that the girl was not injured in any way and appeared in good health. The case was still being investigated.

Once, I was boiled down to the concrete details of everything I could have possibly been. Four, dark blonde, chin-length hair, 40 pounds, 40 inches of a missing girl. My story just ended differently, but I will always wonder what would have happened if it hadn't.

My story could have ended with just a short list of who I was when I disappeared.

Four, dark blonde, chin-length hair, 40 pounds, 40 inches, missing girl.

ACKNOWLEDGEMENTS:

This collection of stories does not happen without Valerie Laken. She's read some version of these many times over many, many years. I walked into her Writer's Workshop as a young college student at UWM, and I have never walked out. I wanted to be a writer, and she showed me what that meant. Respect the word. Respect the story. I'm so glad I listened, and that I then forced her to be my friend.

To my wonderful agent, Lori Galvin. Thank you for supporting my weirdness and for pushing me toward coherence. I'm so lucky to have you in my corner.

To **Rock and a Hard Place**, for believing in me. You have been the best publisher to work with for a fledgling writer. Paul, you are an unbelievable editor. Roger, Jay, Rob, Morgan, Victor, Ashley, Albert, and Susan, the work you do is so important and I'm beyond grateful to be a part of it. Thank you to Heather Garth for the most beautiful cover.

To all the magazines and publishers who picked up these stories in the first place: *Ink Stains*, ***Rock and a Hard Place***, *Tough*, *Apocalypse Confidential*, *Ghost Parachute*, *Shotgun Honey*, *Worcester Review*, *Bristol Noir*, *Bull*, *Chrome Baby*, and *Milwaukee Noir*.

To the teachers. The good ones. We're lost without you.

To the journalists. The good ones. We can't see without you.

To my students. All of you are good. You're everything.

My friends for their support: my momager Tim Hennessey, the Cord, Steve Weddle, the Stinky Butts, Team Brown Out,

Dave, Katrice, Dan, & Joe. Jimmy Boston for coming to almost all of my readings. Kyle and Chris and your beautiful families. Thank goodness we're forever friends. Our neighbors. Our frouple co-parents with all the Ms. My older birthday twin, the Committee Nobody Asked For, Seegs for being the best lil sister a girl could stumble upon later in life. Liz Hein, my biggest hype lady, who is the smartest and fastest reader in the world. Colin for being my biggest hype gentleman. The Christmas at Harts Crew with special shoutouts to Jason Quist for being a brilliant story doctor, and Simon B for telling me once, in my basement, that what I had to say was important. David Weirick, for everything. Jean Vogel for saying yes to being my friend. I love you. Jessica Morman for committing to the bit and being my sister for the last three decades. I love you. To Mary Alexandra Holschbach for continuing to live and continuing to be my heart person. I love you.

To the Thorsons (and all of their assorted last-names): Thank you for welcoming me into your beautiful family. Thank you for raising amazing children, especially that one.

My Franzen (and all of our assorted last-names) Family: Ich liebe dich. It's a miracle we are all here. That our family traveled and settled and from that we have made our homes in each other's hearts, and have kept the most important traditions of love and belief and humor.

To my nieces and nephews! You're all cooler than we will ever be.

To my siblings, Paul, Steph, Ray, and Tommy, for warning me about windowless white vans and the thing outside of my room. For letting me be part of their grownup lives, constantly making me feel like I had four extra parents and four extra friends at the same time. If I'm cool, it's because of you all.

To my mom and dad for telling me stories. For making me feel like stories were important. For telling me their important stories. For making me feel like I had important stories to tell. For giving me everything I needed in this life. For continuing to give me everything I need. I realize, now, that so much of being a parent is giving. I hope I've given you something in return, though it would be an impossible debt to pay. Mom, I still hear you. Dad, you are the best Opa in the world, and without question, the best popsicle.

To Paul, the love of my life, my best friend, the father of my children, the person it is, without question, the easiest to be around. The person who has been making me laugh since high school. I love you. I'm insanely lucky that you continue to put up with me. I'm so glad I picked you.

To my girls, Lucy & Eileen. Make sure you tell each other stories. Make sure you listen. If you have daughters, tell them everything. Make things up, my mother did, and it's fun. Women in our family are fun. And you both are the most fun. Thank you for picking me to be your mommy. I love you more than anything. Forever. Always. My sweetheart babies.

ABOUT THE AUTHOR:

MARY THORSON (IG: @mfranzen88) lives and writes in Milwaukee, Wisconsin. Her short story, "Book of Ruth," was included in *Best American Mystery & Suspense, '24*, edited by Steph Cha and S.A. Cosby. Her short story, "Casadastraphobia," was included in *Best American Mystery & Suspense, '25*, edited by Steph Cha and Don Winslow. Her work has been nominated for *Best American Short Stories*, A Derringer, and a Pushcart Prize. She hangs out with her two feisty daughters, the best husband, and a dog named Pam when she isn't teaching high school English, reading, or writing ghost stories. She is represented by Lori Galvin at Aevitas Creative Management. She is currently working on a novel.